Alex

# Los Gatos of the CIA:

# TANGO WITH A PUMA

## AVENTURAS IN ARGENTINA

¡ Buena suerte, amigo!
Siempre vuele con los
angeles.

*George Arnold*

From an Oral Account by
**Dr. Buford Lewis, Ph.D.**

WWW.CIAcats.com

Illustrated by Jason C. Eckhardt
Translations by Gadylu Espinosa

EAKIN PRESS ⚜ Fort Worth, Texas

This book is a work of fiction, totally the creation of the author's imagination. Actual characters, organizations and locales are used only in a fictional context. Any similarity to real characters or events contained in this manuscript is purely coincidental.

Jason C.
Eckhardt
ILLUSTRATOR
58 Valley View Drive
New Bedford, Ma. 02740
Ph: (401) 635-2762
website - eck-art.net
email -Eckhardtartworks@gmail.com

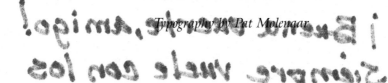

Typography by Pat Molenaar

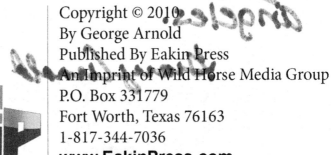

Copyright © 2010
By George Arnold
Published By Eakin Press
An Imprint of Wild Horse Media Group
P.O. Box 331779
Fort Worth, Texas 76163
1-817-344-7036
www.EakinPress.com
1 2 3 4 5 6 7 8 9
ISBN-10: 1-934645-96-6
ISBN-13: 978-1-934645-96-3
Library of Congress Control Number 2009940514

# Readers' Praise for
# *Tango with a Puma*

## Student readers offer their thoughts

"*So good that when I see my cats I think of them as secret agents.*"

"*It was just perfect. Nothing (about it) was horrible.*"

"*I liked it a lot. It was very entertaining and interesting. Oh, and now I think of all cats as secret agents.*"

"*I'm not into animal books (but) this was a good book.*"

## Adult readers react to *Tango with a Puma*

"*Arnold's latest cat caper is sure to entertain children and their parents, too.*"

"*It's like nothing I've ever read before.*"

"*Not only is the book fun to read, but also it will make readers want to hop the next flight to Argentina - cats, dogs and pig in tow.*"

"*Once again, George Arnold has scored with a book that adults can delight in without guilt or embarrassment when they share it with children. And it's pretty darn sneaky about teaching children Spanish when they read it to themselves. Of course, that applies to adults who don't speak or read Spanish, too.*"

*"The character Carlos the Puma was well developed, fleshed out, and interesting, at least to an adult reader like me."*

*"Loved it! Love the title. Action and suspense get my attention, and this one has both!"*

*"A fun and easy way to learn Spanish phrases and vocabulary."*

*"Turns what would be a simple children's story into an interesting way to inspire interest and teach a foreign language."*

*"The story, while captivating, becomes a valuable aid to learning a foreign language. This unique approach is a masterful stroke in marketing."*

*"Reading it was fun."*

*"An easy and fun way to introduce young people to the Spanish language."*

*"It kept me guessing where the next twist and funny remarks were going to come from."*

*"¡Un milagro! The action scenes were SO good. The book held my interest throughout."*

*"I love the kindergarten humor of the little kittens. Perhaps I'm a five-year-old at heart . . . or the writer is, to capture it so well."*

*"I really enjoyed trying to figure out the Spanish words . . . and learning more about Argentina."*

*"I enjoyed very much—and love the idea—of cats and a dancing pig saving the day."*

*For*
*Hannah, Mariel, Julianne, and Liam,*
*and cats and cat lovers everywhere.*
*And for Lucy Jennings and David Berkman,*
*patrons extraordinaire.*


*In memory of*
*Virginia Gholson Messer*
*and*
*Tommy Messer*
*Friends, Mentors, Publishers*

# BOOKS BY GEORGE ARNOLD
## From Sunbelt Media

### The Cats of the C.I.A. Fiction Series

*Get Fred-X*: *The Cats of the C.I.A.*

*Hunt for Fred-X*: *Los Gatos of the C.I.A.*

*Fred-X Rising*: *I Gatti of the C.I.A.*

*Tango with a Puma*: *Los Gatos of the C.I.A.*

COMING SOON: *Eiffel's Trifles & Troubles*: *Les Chats of the C.I.A.*

### Nonfiction books for readers of all ages

*Growing Up Simple*: *An Irreverent Look at Kids in the 1950s*

*Chick Magnates, Ayatollean Televangelist, & A Pig Farmer's Beef*: *Inside the Sometimes Hilarious World of Advertising*

*BestSeller*: *Must-Read Author's Guide to Successfully Selling Your Book*

**For more information, visit the author's Web site:**
**www.CIAcats.com**

Los Gatos of the CIA:

# TANGO WITH A PUMA

## AVENTURAS IN ARGENTINA

# * Contents *

# * Author's Note *

Vowels and vowel combinations are pronounced differently in Spanish than they are in English. As you read this book, if you are interested in the correct pronunciation of the Spanish words, please turn to the Glossary near the back of the book. You will find all the words and phrases there, along with a guide to help you pronounce them correctly. The pronunciation will be as you would hear Spanish spoken in Argentina, which differs a little from that of other Central and South American countries.

# \* Cast of Characters \*

STARRING

**Buzzer Louis Giaccomazza**: Renowned retired director of operations of the C.I.A.—Cats-In-Action. Black-and-white tuxedo cat from the Hill Country of Texas, known among law enforcement officials worldwide for his clever and effective lifelong fight against bad guys. Knighted at Buckingham Palace by Queen Elizabeth. Now Sir Buzzer.

**Cincinnati the dancing pig**: Buzzer's closest friend and former C.I.A. contract operative. Owner of 114 dance studios throughout the Midwest. Flies his own sleek twin fanjet Sabreliner (*The Flying Pig Machine*) with a long-distance pack. Learning to speak Spanish.

**Dusty Louise Giaccomazza**: Buzzer's pretty but somewhat impatient younger sister. A gray tabby who always wants the answer. Right now. Often before she knows the question. Dusty is learning to be a pilot. She trades Spanish lessons with Cincinnati in return for flying lessons.

**Luigi Panettone Giaccomazza**: Hilarious tiny orange tabby prankster. Baby brother of Buzzer Louis and Dusty Louise.

**Luisa Manicotti Giaccomazza**: Wise, thoughtful and seriously funny little orange tabby. Luisa is Luigi's twin sister.

**La Capitán Paloma Pérez**: Division chief of the Argentinean state police for the region surrounding Buenos Aires. Tall and thin, she is a direct descendant of the Mayan civilization on the Mexican Yucatán. In charge of the four-country search for Carlos the Puma.

**Teniente Guillermo C. Trovarsi**: The right-hand assistant to Capitán Paloma. Guillermo is a young, new detective. His mother is Argentinean, his father from Italy. The teniente asks everyone to call him "Chuck." He is learning to speak English.

**Sargento Jaime Espinosa**: A hotel bellman who has another, much more important job.

**Capitán Ramos**: Shady master of a 39-foot river trawler, *El Meteoro*. An Argentinean from Buenos Aires, he plies the Amazon River carrying passengers, mail and freight. This time he has only one passenger, a very dangerous passenger whose name he doesn't know: Carlos the Puma.

**Carlos the Puma**[1]: Infamous international terrorist. A mean motor scooter. Following his capture at the Sheraton Hotel in Buenos Aires four years

---

1. Cougar

ago by Buzzer Louis and Cincinnati the dancing pig, Carlos has been jailed in an awful prison near the headwaters of the Amazon River in Brasil, a place so terrible and so remote that a prisoner has never escaped. Until now.

**Dr. Buford Lewis, Ph.D.**: Foreman of Buzzer's little ranch in the Texas hills. Only known Labrador retriever with a doctor of philosophy degree. Holder of the Rin Tin Tin Chair of Literature and professor emeritus at the University of California at Barkley.

**Bogart-BOGART**: Dr. Buford's younger brother and assistant ranch foreman. Often lost in deep thought, he is very, very smart—a real thinker.

**Uncontacted Indian Tribe**: A tribe of indigenous natives, led by El Jefe[2] Gris, deep in the remote rainforests of Brasil. Knowing nothing of the world beyond a few mile radius of their remote site, they befriend Carlos the Puma, thinking him a god because of his 'magic fire stick.'

**Basko Conde**: A large Rottweiler—member of the K-9 corps of the PFA, *Policía Federal de Argentina*.

---

2. The chief

# * Introduction *
# One Owl Down.
# One Puma to Go.

As our story begins, Buzzer Louis and his best friend, Cincinnati the dancing pig, with the help of Buzzer's siblings—the pretty gray tabby, Dusty Louise, and the tiny orange tabby twins, Luigi and Luisa—have just finished tracking down and finally putting a stop to the catnabbing habits of Fred-X. You see, Fred-X is a big spotted owl whose habit of grabbing cats and flying off with them, to sell them as slaves, had to be stopped.

First, the little band of crime fighters tracked Fred-X down in Mexico. Just as they had accepted congratulations, and even some awards, from the president of Mexico for their work, Fred-X somehow escaped from a *Yucatán* jail. He winged his way to Italy, where he was joined by his German girlfriend, Frieda-K, and the greedy Cardinal *Umberto Ucello* from the Vatican. The three of them started grabbing Italian cats to take to a one-armed captain of a ship in Venice, who in turn would sell them into the Tunisian slave market. So our crime-fighting team had to track Fred-X down once again.

This time in Italy.

With Fred-X now safely in the custody of Interpol and the Italian *carabinieri* (state police), the team is headed home from Italy in Cincinnati's beautiful twin fanjet Sabreliner, *The Flying Pig Machine*. After a brief stop for fuel and some fun in Newfoundland, they are over Ohio and headed to the Texas hills when a call comes in on Buzzer's satellite telephone from Socks, head of the C.I.A. in the White House basement.

"The Brazilian and Argentinean authorities are looking for you," Socks tells Buzzer Louis. "*Carlos* the Puma has escaped from prison, and they think he's headed for *Buenos Aires*."

Buzzer and his team had been expecting to take a little time off for some rest—and to return to the sedate life of farming on their little ranch. Buzzer and Cincinnati had captured *Carlos* four years earlier, by staging a wine tasting and tango contest in the *Buenos Aires* Sheraton's ballroom, on the hotel's twenty-third floor. And *Carlos* had been sent to prison for a very long time.

Seven European countries are now standing by to bring *Carlos* to trial for various terrorist acts—fire bombings, assassinations, stealing state secrets—if he should ever be released from the South American prison.

So, even as tired as they are, Buzzer and Cincinnati

know it is their duty to pitch in and help capture *Carlos* once again. After all, nobody anywhere knows more about *Carlos* and his tricks than Buzzer Louis and Cincinnati the dancing pig do.

"We'll call *Buenos Aires* as soon as we land in the Hill Country," Buzzer tells Socks. "If they need us, of course we'll go and help."

He knows in his heart of hearts that they will be off again, and quickly.

Dusty Louise is piloting *The Flying Pig Machine*. The mischievous Luigi and Luisa are napping, following a long stint of their favorite airplane game—"jumpseat." Buzzer and Cincinnati, resigned to another exciting assignment, take out the dancing pig's maps and charts and begin plotting a course from the Hill Country Intergalactic Airport to *Buenos Aires*.

Let the fun begin.

Again.

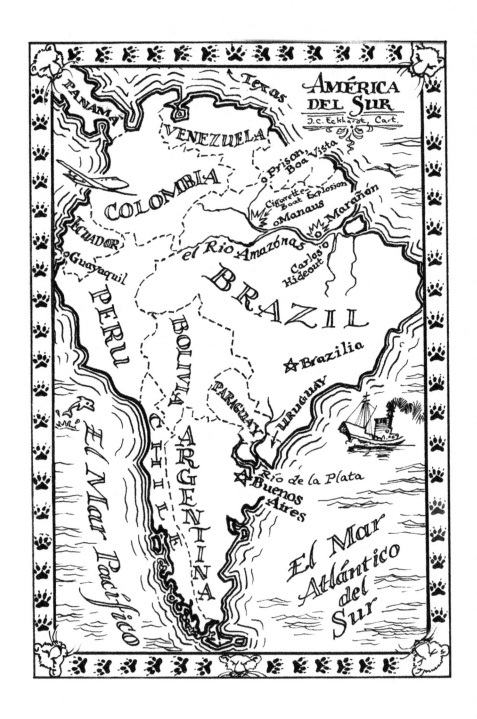

# Part One

## Here We Go.
## One More Time.

"*Carlos* the Puma is not only dangerous, but also very smart. We tricked him once, four years ago. Tricking him again won't be as easy. We're in for a real battle. Bet on it."

—Buzzer Louis
Retired DO/CIA

# * Chapter 1 *
## Home Again—*Por Poquito Tiempo*[1]

Luigi Panettone Giaccomazza and his tiny orange tabby twin sister, Luisa Manicotti Giaccomazza, woke with a start. The screech of tires dropping lightly onto the concrete runway of the Hill Country Intergalactic Airport (HCIA) was just noise enough to cause them to sit up and begin rubbing the sleep from their eyes.

Cincinnati the dancing pig had floated his sleek fanjet Sabreliner—*The Flying Pig Machine*—ever so softly onto runway three. A perfect landing, as usual for the dancing pig, a pilot most excellent. A perfect ending to a long, quiet flight home from Italy.

And owl catching.

"You take the stick," Cincinnati said quickly to his co-pilot in training, the twins' big sister, Dusty Louise. Dusty,

1. In Spanish, "briefly"

*3*

a pretty gray tabby, was learning to fly airplanes, trading flying lessons from Cincinnati for Spanish lessons. You see, she spoke excellent Spanish.

"Taxi over to the parking ramp next to the terminal, Dusty, and I'll open the door and jump down to set the wheel chocks. We won't be here long enough to worry about a hangar, I think," Cincinnati said. "Call the tower and ask them to send the Chevron truck to fill up the tanks. We're almost dry, and we have a ways to go pretty quickly." He strolled to the front door to open it and let down the stairs.

"Did you hear that, Luigi?" Luisa popped wide-awake and shook her tiny brother. "Cincinnati said we won't be here very long. What do you suppose that means, *fratello*?"[2]

"I don't know, Luisa." Luigi was waking up slowly. "Buzzer, what did Cincinnati mean about 'not being here very long?'" Luigi poked at his big brother, Buzzer Louis, the last member of the traveling group. A black-and-white tuxedo cat, Buzzer was so used to flying that Cincinnati's feather-light landings seldom woke him if he was napping.

"Yes, Buzzer, what did Cincinnati mean?" Luisa chimed in. She stared at Buzzer's eyes as they slowly opened. Little Luisa was almost as curious as Luigi. And she was almost as impatient as her big sister, Dusty Louise.

Buzzer looked at the tiny twins. "Socks called a couple of hours ago, guys," he said slowly. "We have a problem to help solve in South America, I think."

"What problem?" the twins shouted in unison.

---

2. Fratello is the word for "brother" in Italian.

Before Buzzer could answer, Dusty braked the little jet to an abrupt, rocking stop. She shut down power and the two jet engines whined to a silent standstill. Dusty was still learning and had not yet mastered Cincinnati's light touch on the brakes.

"Home again, home again, jiggety-jog," Cincinnati announced as he turned the big lever to open the door and let down the stairs. "Sit tight for *un momento, por favor*,[3] and I'll set the chocks and get somebody to call us a taxi."

"We're a taxi!" Luigi shouted, to Luisa's delight, as Cincinnati tripped lightly down the stairs. He moved as only a graceful dancer could, landing lightly on the tarmac. He headed for a small compartment under the left wing, where the triangle shaped blocks called "chocks" were stored.

Dusty Louise stepped out of the cockpit, her flight's shutdown checklist complete. She had turned off every switch and light up front. "Luigi, you are such a little pill," Dusty said in response to her baby brother's taxi remark. "I'll be glad when you grow up some more," she said.

Luisa turned to Luigi and spoke quietly into his ear. "Watch out, Luigi. Dusty needs a pill right now, herself. Just as she usually does. She might gobble you down with a big glass of water." Luisa snickered at the mental picture of Dusty trying to take Luigi as a pill.

Luigi and Luisa had an unusual relationship with Dusty. They thought she was wired a little too tight. Her efforts to make them behave and mature were, in the minds of the

---

3. In Spanish, "a moment, please." (Dusty is teaching Cincinnati to speak Spanish.)

twins, a tad heavy-handed. After all, the two of them went to Sister Mary Consecration's kindergarten. They believed they got all the instruction they needed there, from the good sister they called Sister Mary "Cannonball." Or sometimes, if they wanted to be especially mischievous, Sister Mary "Constipation."

"What about it?" Luigi demanded, shifting subjects as only he could do. He asked his out-of-the-blue question to his big brother, Buzzer Louis.

Puzzled, Buzzer said, "What about what, Luigi?"

"About my question, of course. What else?" Luigi pressed on. Why couldn't Buzzer and Dusty ever pay attention to a simple conversation? he wondered.

"I'm lost, Luigi" Buzzer confessed. "What are you talking about?"

Luisa jumped in to try to unscramble Luigi's little puzzle. "He means about not being here very long, you know? Like, why are we not going to be here long? And where are we going this time?" Luisa smiled and batted her long eyelashes. She had learned that smiling and batting eyelashes made her look cute.

It also made Buzzer and Dusty pay attention.

Dusty strolled up to where her three siblings were sitting just in time to hear the end of Luisa's explanation.

"What in the world are the two of them talking about now?" she asked Buzzer.

"You don't know either?" he said. "I thought maybe Cincinnati had told you."

"Nobody's told me a thing. Cincinnati was teaching me how to use the autopilot on a long trip of more than 8,000 kilometers. And I was teaching him how to conjugate Spanish verbs. Nobody said anything specific to me about leaving here again. What's going on, anyway?"

Dusty was her usual impatient self. This time, though, she had Luigi and Luisa just as curious. And Luisa, at least, just as impatient.

"All clear. Come on down. Dusty, you come out last. Turn out the cabin lights and shut the door, please. I have a cab coming to take us to the *Tenutina*,"[4] Cincinnati called up from the ground below. "We've got to get to your house. Make some long distance phone calls. Do some serious plotting with my maps and charts. Which reminds me. Buzzer, please grab my black captain's bag. The one with the laptop and all the charts. Thanks."

He waited for the rest of the crime-fighting team to join him on the tarmac.

He stood below wondering why the others hadn't come out the door. Then Cincinnati heard a ruckus coming from *The Flying Pig Machine*'s cabin. It sounded as though everyone up there was talking at once. He could hear snatches of phrases.

Luigi was talking. Luisa was talking. Dusty was shouting frantically.

Finally he heard Buzzer Louis scream, "QUIET! All of you!"

Cincinnati was taken aback. He had never, ever heard the soft-spoken Buzzer Louis even raise his voice, let alone scream like that.

---

4. The name of Buzzer Louis's little ranch. It means 'little farm' in Italian.

Cincinnati heard a low mumbling. Then silence again.

Luigi and Luisa, shocked, quietly came through the door and trudged solemnly down the stairs to join Cincinnati. It was obvious to the dancing pig that the twins had never heard such a command from their big brother, either.

Buzzer was next. He looked confused and perplexed. Cincinnati thought the one most surprised by Buzzer's outburst was the tuxedo cat himself. Buzzer looked at Cincinnati as he walked across the apron. He shrugged his shoulders and raised his front paws with both elbows at his sides as if to say, "Did I just do what I think I did?"

At the foot of the stairs, Dusty moved a lever to cause the stairs to go back up and the door to shut. She handed Cincinnati a set of keys to *The Flying Pig Machine*. Then she stood, frozen. Not moving a muscle. Not looking right or left. She was in a trance.

Cincinnati the dancing pig looked at the quiet group gathered next to him. A taxi pulled up on the other side of the fence that separated the parking ramp from the terminal.

"That's our cab," the dancing pig said, adding cautiously, "I don't suppose anybody wants to tell me what in the world just happened up there?" He glanced up toward the cabin.

"Not now, please," Buzzer said. "Let's just get to the house. Once we get there I can say it all once. To Dusty. To Luigi and Luisa. To Dr. Buford Lewis and his very smart brother Bogart-BOGART, the foremen of our little ranch."

Buzzer looked at each of his siblings. He looked at his best friend, Cincinnati, and said, *"Lo siento. Yo estoy cansado.*

*También mi hermano pequeño y mis dos hermanas lo están con tantas preguntas simultáneamente. Lo siento, también, amigos míos."*[5]

Then he turned and walked slowly toward the taxi, calling over his shoulder, *"Vámonos a casa.*[6] *Tenemos mucho trabajo por hacer."*[7]

The four cats and the dancing pig stepped quietly into the waiting taxi as the driver hoisted Cincinnati's black pilot's case and the twins' *dos mochilas*[8] into the trunk.

Two men in a Chevron truck began filling the fuel tanks of *The Flying Pig Machine* as the cab pulled away from the terminal at HCIA for the short trip to the *Tenutina*. Maybe, just maybe, Dusty and the twins would get their questions answered soon.

*What do you think caused the usually soft-spoken Buzzer Louis to raise his voice so? Why do you think he suddenly began speaking Spanish? Do you have any idea why Cincinnati didn't tell Dusty about* Carlos *the Puma's escaping from the awful prison in Brazil? Do you think Buzzer, Cincinnati, and the gang will have to end up going to South America? What about Dr. Buford Lewis, Ph.D., and his very smart brother Bogart-BOGART? Will they get to go, too?*

---

5. "I'm sorry. I'm tired. Also, my little brother and two sisters are a bit tiresome with so many questions at once. I'm sorry again, my friends."
6. "Let's go to our house."
7. "We have a lot of work to do."
8. Two backpacks.

# Aprendamos a Hablar en Español
## by Dusty Louise

At the end of each chapter, I—Dusty Louise—the pretty gray tabby who is also (I admit it) sometimes impatient, but who speaks Spanish *muy bien*[9] and now even flies airplanes, will write a little vocabulary to help you learn to speak some more Spanish. Here are some numbers to help you get started. *Adelante!*[10]

## NUMBERS

| In English | In Spanish | Say It Like This |
| --- | --- | --- |
| one | uno | OO-noh |
| two | dos | DOSE |
| three | tres | trace |
| four | cuatro | KWAH-troh |
| five | cinco | SEEN-coh |
| six | seis | SAYCE |
| seven | siete | see-ET-eh |
| eight | ocho | OH-cho |
| nine | nueve | noo-AY-veh |
| ten | diez | dee-AYZ |
| eleven | once | OHN-say |
| twelve | doce | DOH-say |
| thirteen | trece | TRAY-seh |
| fourteen | catorce | cah-TOHR-say |
| fifteen | quince | keen-SAY |
| sixteen | dieciséis | dee-AYZ-ee-SAYCE |

9. Very well.
10. "Forward" or "Onward."

| | | |
|---|---|---|
| seventeen | diecisiete | dee-AYZ-ee-see-ET-eh |
| eighteen | dieciocho | dee-AYZ-ee-OH-cho |
| nineteen | diecinueve | dee-AYZ-ee-noo-AY-veh |
| twenty | veinte | VAYN-teh |
| twenty-one | veintiuno | vayn-tee-OO-noh |
| twenty-two | veintidós | vayn-tee-DOHS |
| twenty-three | veintitrés | vayn-tee-TRACE |
| twenty-four | veinticuatro | vayn-tee-KWAH-troh |
| twenty-five | veinticinco | vayn-tee-SEEN-coh |
| thirty | treinta | TRAY-en-tah |
| forty | cuarenta | kwahr-EN-tah |
| fifty | cincuenta | seen-KWIHN-tah |
| sixty | sesenta | say-SIHN-tah |
| seventy | setenta | say-TIHN-tah |
| eighty | ochenta | oh-CHIN-tah |
| ninety | noventa | noh-VIHN-tah |
| one hundred | cien | see-IHN |
| two hundred | doscientos | doh-see-IHN-tohs |
| three hundred | trescientos | tray-see-IHN-tohs |
| four hundred | cuatrocientos | KWAH-troh-see-IHN-tohs |
| five hundred | quinientos | KEEN-ee-IHN-tohs |
| six hundred | seiscientos | SAYZ-see-IHN-tohs |
| seven hundred | setecientos | SET-eh-see-IHN-tohs |
| eight hundred | ochocientos | OH-cho-see-IHN-tohs |
| nine hundred | novecientos | NOH-vay-see-IHN-tohs |
| one thousand | mil | MEEL |
| one hundred thousand | cien mil | see-EHN-MEEL |
| one million | un million | OON-mee-YOHN |
| one billion | mil milliones | MEEL-mee-YOH-nehs |

# * Chapter 2 *
# Carlos the Puma–
# Terrorista Suelto[1]

The taxi pulled up to the new stone ranch house with the big red barn out back. Buzzer Louis' *Tenutina*. Dr. Buford Lewis, Ph.D., and his very smart brother Bogart-BOGART, a pair of Labrador retrievers who worked as foremen for Buzzer's farming activities, stepped out onto the long front porch to greet the returning travelers.

"Hi Buzzer, Cincinnati, Dusty, Luigi, Luisa," Bogart-BOGART said. "Welcome home. Hard to believe you've only been gone five days. Seems like a month to me."

Dr. Buford stepped toward Buzzer. "Buzz, did Socks reach you? There have been six or seven calls for you since early this morning. Do you know who's calling? And what they want?" Buford asked privately. "Also, what's wrong

---

1. Terrorist on the loose.

with Dusty and the twins? They look like something scared the fun out of them."

Buzzer Louis turned his back to his family and faced Buford. "I think I just yelled at Dusty and the twins. I must have scared them. I know I scared me. It'll be all right after I have the chance to tell all of you what's happening. And yes, Buford, I have a pretty good idea who's been calling, and I think I know what they want. Did anybody leave a name and international number?"

Dusty, Cincinnati, and the twins trudged into the house, trailed by Bogart-BOGART, who was trying to get them to tell him about their adventures in Italy. He found they were strangely quiet, though. Not nearly as talkative as usual.

Cincinnati herded everybody into the great room in front of the big fireplace. "There's news Buzzer and I need to tell you about, folks," he said. "Let's all get together so we can all hear it one time. I want us all to hear—and know—exactly the same thing. Buzzer, you want to fill everyone in?"

"Thanks, Cincinnati," Buzzer Louis began. "First, I want to thank everyone for the excellent work we just completed in Italy. Fred-X, you will be happy to know—" Buzzer looked at Dr. Buford Lewis and Bogart-BOGART— "is locked away in an Italian jail, along with his German girlfriend, Frieda-K. Interpol and the Italian state police— the *carabinieri*—will return Fred-X to Mexico to stand trial. He won't be stealing any more cats for a long, long time.

"Next, I want to say I'm sorry to Dusty Louise and Luigi and Luisa. I'm afraid I yelled at the three of you today. I

apologize for that. Here's what you were asking about when
. . . well, when I kind of exploded." Buzzer looked sad.

"It's okay, big brother," said Luigi. "Just tell us what's
happened."

Luisa chimed in, "And where we are going next."

"And when we're going," added Dusty Louise.

All three smiled at their brother, and he felt a little better.

Buzzer looked at Cincinnati. "You know the whole story,
Cincinnati. Would you care to tell everyone what we think
is about to happen?"

Cincinnati stood and walked over to the hearth of the
big stone fireplace, where he sat down and began. "It's really pretty simple. Socks called Buzzer about three hours
ago as we were over Ohio on our way back here. She said
the Argentinean and Brazilian authorities are trying to
reach him—because that terrible international terrorist,
*Carlos* the Puma, has escaped from prison. A snitch at the
prison 'way up near the headwaters of the Amazon River
told the warden that *Carlos* plans to slip into *Buenos Aires*."

Cincinnati looked to Buzzer to see if he wanted to add
anything. Buzzer nodded and said, "Go ahead."

"*Buenos Aires* was where we last saw *Carlos* the Puma. At
first he was disguised as a Chinese shoe salesman,"
Cincinnati continued. "But Buzzer and I tricked him into
entering a big wine tasting and tango contest. We wrapped
him up there outside the Sheraton Hotel and handed him
over to the authorities. He went to jail—sentenced to a
long, long term. That was four years ago. But you all know
that story, right?"

"Tell us again! Pleeeze!" It was Luigi, who loved a good story.

"Yes, Cincinnati. Tell us the story again," Luisa joined in.

"Just a minute, you two," Dusty said sternly. "Before we do any long-winded storytelling . . . No offense, Cincinnati," she added, turning to the dancing pig, "I want to know exactly where are we going. And when."

Classic Dusty Louise: Impatient to a fault. Wanting answers, right now.

Buzzer winked at his gray tabby sister. "Dusty, those classes on being more patient at the Hill Country Junior College aren't working too well today, are they? I'm sure everybody wants to know the same things. Right now I don't know the exact answers, though. First I have to return some of these calls to South America. And then call Socks to clear our plans with her. Give me an hour, okay?" Then I'll tell you what I think's really going to happen."

"Fine," Dusty answered, and turned to Luigi and Luisa. "Meantime, you two little scamps go to your room and unpack *los recuerdos de Italia en sus mochilas*.[2]

Get those *mochilas* ready for another trip. We're going someplace for sure, you two. And it sounds like you may need to start paying attention to me translating Spanish."

Dusty gave the tiny prankster twins a smug look, as if she held some power over them.

"Oh, no!" Luisa rolled her eyes. "Here we go again."

"*Verdad, hermanita*,"[3] Luigi agreed. "She really thinks

2. the souvenirs from Italy in your backpacks.
3. "True, my little sister."

she's the only person in the world who understands Spanish and English."

"And she's still not happy that we got to be the interpreters in Italy, don't forget, Luigi," Luisa whispered. "Even though we know a lot more Italian than she does."

Dusty Louise noticed the two tiny orange tabbies whispering. She walked over to them and demanded, "I asked you two to go do what? What? Answer me!"

"Empty the souvenirs out of our backpacks," Luisa answered, shrugging her shoulders and wondering what this little scene was really all about.

Luigi couldn't resist adding, laughing out loud. "Mine's a mess. It's full of ice cream—*gelato di Venezia*[4]—and it's all melted and sloshing around in there. I need a jar to pour it in."

"Then you can stick it back in the freezer," Luisa laughed. "Or just drink it."

Cincinnati the dancing pig saved the two pranksters from the wrath of their big sister. "Dusty, while Buzzer's calling South America and Socks, let's you and I look at some potential flight plans from here to say, oh—maybe *Buenos Aires*. Just in case, don't you see?"

A light went on in Dusty's head. "Does this have anything to do with why you were showing me how to use the autopilot on very long flights, flights over eight thousand kilometers, Cincinnati?" She smiled, realizing she had a clue before the twins knew anything. And then she wondered why in the world she was jealous of those two little ragamuffins.

---

4. (in Italian) ice cream from Venice.

Dusty joined the dancing pig as Cincinnati opened his black captain's case, plugged in his laptop to recharge and began spreading charts and maps out flat on the dining room table.

"I think it's about five thousand miles—eight thousand kilometers," Cincinnati said, mostly to himself. Looking up at Dusty Louise, he added, "We'll need to make one stop. We could make two. I don't like to go much beyond five thousand kilometers—a little over three thousand miles. It's not just the distance and the fuel reserve, but also the time. Need to get out and stretch your legs every so often, know what I mean? We dancers don't want to get leg cramps, do we?"

He spread another map on the tabletop. "Let's see what we've got here. Look it over. I'm going to join Buzzer for a minute. Be right back." As Luigi and Luisa hoisted their backpacks and scampered off to put away their Italian souvenirs, Buzzer Louis was in his office with Dr. Buford Lewis and Bogart-BOGART. Cincinnati slipped in quietly.

"Here are the calls, Buzzer," Dr. Buford said, handing Buzzer a pad with a couple of names and several phone numbers on it. "Looks like this lady *La Capitán Paloma Pérez*,[5] with the Argentine federal police, called three times. And this *Teniente Guillermo Trovarsi*[6] also called a couple of times. I think he must work for La Capitán."

Buzzer Louis was mumbling to himself, thinking out loud. "Let's see. It's about four o'clock in the afternoon here. I think *Buenos Aires* is at least two time zones east of

5. Captain *Paloma* (Dove) *Pérez*
6. Lieutenant *Guillermo* (William) *Trovarsi*

us. Maybe three. So it should be six or seven o'clock in the evening there. Let's just see if *la capitán* is still in her office." He punched up the speakerphone and began to dial, reading the numbers aloud. "*Cero-uno-uno, cinco-cuatro, seis-siete-seis, ocho-cero-tres, cero-cero-nueve-dos.*"[7]

Buzzer, Buford and Bogart-BOGART heard a series of electronic tones and clicks. A phone began to ring.

Then came an answer—or rather an answering machine message: "*Hola. Listo. Le llama La Capitán Paloma. Si usted es el Señor Buzzer Louis de los Estados Unidos, favor de telefonearme a la casa—cero-uno-uno, cinco-cuatro, seis-siete-seis, nueve-cero-nueve, ocho-tres-uno-cero. Gracias, Señor Gato Muy Famoso.*"[8]

"What did she say, Buzzer?" Dr. Buford wanted to know.

Bogart-BOGART, always thinking, answered, "I think she wants you to call her at home. Right, Buzz?"

"Right you are, Bogart-BOGART," Buzzer answered.

So the world-famous tuxedo cat from the Texas Hill Country punched up the speakerphone again, and began to dial the *capitán's* home phone number.

*What do you think* la capitán *wants to talk to Buzzer about? Will she be home? Can Cincinnati and Dusty find a safe and simple route to* Buenos Aires *without having to make too many stops along the way? What about the twins'* mochilas? *Is Luigi's backpack really full of melted ice cream from* Venezia? *Is Italian gelato really the souvenir he brought back with him?*

---

7. An international phone number: 011-54-676-803-0092.
8. "Hello. Ready. This is Captain *Paloma*. If you are Mr. Buzzer Louis from the United States, please call me at home—011-54-676-909-8310. Thank you, Mr. very famous cat."

# Aprendamos a Hablar en Español

by Dusty Louise

Are you practicing your numbers from the last chapter? Good. *Muy bien, amigos. Ahora, vamos a aprender muchos colores.*[9]

## COLORS

| In English | In Spanish | Say It Like This |
| --- | --- | --- |
| Red | *Rojo* | RO-hoh |
| Blue | *Azul* | ah-SZOOL |
| White | *Blanco* | BLAHN-coh |
| Green | *Verde* | VAIR-deh |
| Yellow | *Amarillo* | ah-mah-REE-zho |
| Orange | *Anaranjado* | Ah-nah-rahn-HAH-doh |
| Brown | (in Argentina) | |
| | *Marrón* | *Mah-ROHN* |
| | (in other countries) | |
| | *Café* | Cah-FEY |
| Black | *Negro* | NAY-groh |
| Violet | *Violeta* | vee-oh-LEHT-ah |
| Rose | *Rosa* | ROH-sah |
| Gray | *Gris* | GREESE |
| Silver | *Plata* | PLAH-tah |
| Gold | *Oro* | OHR-oh |
| Maroon | *Granate* | grah-NAH-teh |
| Indigo | *Índigo* | EEN-dee-goh |
| Lavender | *Lavanda* | lah-VAHN-dah |
| Pink | *Rosado* | roh-SAH-doh |
| Purple | *Púrpura* | PUHR-poo-rah |
| Sepia | *Sepia* | SAY-pee-ah |
| Turquoise | *Turquesa* | toor-KAY-sah |

---

9. Very good, friends. Now we're going to learn many colors.

# * Chapter 3 *
# Vámonos a América del Sur[1]

*En la Casa de la Capitán Pérez—Buenos Aires, Argentina*[2]

*Teniente Guillermo Trovarsi* and *Capitán Paloma Pérez* sat by the telephone in the living room of the *capitán*'s apartment in *Buenos Aires*. They were sipping steaming cups of *yerba mate*, a strong green herbal tea favored by Argentineans, Uruguayans and Brazilians.

Setting down his cup, the *teniente* asked his boss a question. "*¿Por qué el Señor Buzzer Louis no le telefonea desde los Estados Unidos? ¿O tal vez su amigo el gato Norteamericano, el Señor Cincinnati, el cerdo bailarín?*"[3]

*La Capitán Paloma Pérez* answered, "*No sé, teniente. No entiendo mucho de los vecinos Norteamericanos. Algunos de los*

---

1. Let's go to South America!
2. In Captain Pérez's house in Buenos Aires, Argentina
3. "Why doesn't this Mr. Buzzer Louis from the United States call you? Or maybe his friend, Cincinnati the dancing pig?"

*humanos son extraños, por cierto. Tal vez los gatos y los cerdos del norte también lo sean. ¿Verdad, teniente?*[4]

*"Pero son detectives muy competentes—el gato y su amigo el cerdo. Muy competentes sin duda, teniente,"* she added.[5]

*"Pues, ama a tu prójimo, capitán,"*[6] the *teniente* added with a wink and a sly smile.

Just as he finished speaking, the phone next to the *capitána* chirped twice. She picked it up. *"Hola. Aquí está la capitán Paloma. ¿Quién es, por favor?"*[7]

The *capitán* listened a moment and then responded, *"Ah, Señor Buzzer Louis. Bueno, señor. ¿Habla usted Español?"*[8]

Again, she listened briefly. *"¿No lo habla bien? Entonces, no hay problema. Mi ayudante, el teniente Guillermo Trovarsi, habla bien Inglés. Aquí está el teniente."*[9]

With that, she handed the phone to the *teniente.*

He spoke into the receiver, *"Hola, Señor Gato Norteamericano. Lo atiende el Teniente Trovarsi."*[10] Then he slipped into the English he was studying at the local university on weekends. "Call me Chuck, please, sir."

He listened a minute and then said, "Yes, it's true. My *apellido*—you would say 'surname,' I think—is Italian. My father came here from Italy, along with many Italians of his

4. "I don't know, Lieutenant. I don't understand these North American neighbors very well. Some of the humans are strange, for sure. Maybe also the cats and pigs from up north? Right, Lieutenant?"
5. "But they are very capable detectives, the cat and his friend, the pig. Very capable detectives, without doubt, Lieutenant."
6. "Well, love your neighbor, captain."
7. "Hello. This is Captain Paloma. Who is this, please?"
8. "Ah, Mr. Buzzer Louis. Do you speak Spanish?"
9. "You don't speak it well? Then, that's not a problem. My assistant, Lieutenant Guillermo Trovarsi speaks English well. Here's the lieutenant."
10. "Hello, Mr. North American cat. Lieutenant Trovarsi here."

generation. And my mother is Argentinean. And the English name for *Guillermo* is William. But my middle name is Carlos. So everyone calls me 'Chuck.'"

*Capitán Paloma Pérez* wanted to hear both sides of the conversation, so she turned on the speakerphone. She could speak more and better English than she would admit, though not as well as Chuck.

Buzzer Louis was talking. "My good friend and fellow criminal catcher, Cincinnati the dancing pig, is here with me for a moment, *teniente* Chuck. We just got back less than an hour ago from Italy."

*"Hola, Señor Cerdo Bailarín,"*[11] *Capitán Paloma* said.

*"Hola, capitán y teniente,"*[12] Cincinnati said, adding, "Buzzer's sister, Dusty Louise, is teaching me Spanish."

Buzzer spoke up. "We understand you have perhaps a terrible international terrorist headed your way. *Carlos* the Puma. Is that right?"

"Yes, Mr. Louis," *teniente* Chuck answered. "*Carlos*—I think you know him well, no? He dug a tunnel and escaped from that awful maximum-security prison in Brazil. The one located almost at the mouth of the Amazon River. That was yesterday morning. One of the Brazilian prison's—how would you say?—'informants,' perhaps?"

---

11. "Hello, Mr. Dancing Pig."
12. "Hello, Captain and Lieutenant."

"We call them 'snitches', Chuck," Cincinnati said.

"Right. A snitch. He told the warden that *Carlos* was bragging that he would be the first ever to escape—and live, that is. And he said he'd be in *Buenos Aires* within five days." Sounding doubtful, *Teniente* Chuck added, "I do not believe that is possible."

Cincinnati spoke up. "Don't doubt *Carlos*, Chuck. He's very smart. He has a bunch of friends in the underworld, and a ton of resources. If he said he'll be in *Buenos Aires* in five days, I—for one—would expect him to be there. In three more days."

Cincinnati continued, "Sorry, but I have to get back to helping Dusty Louise with the maps and charts. We expect we'll need to come there right away. Please excuse me. Or, as Dusty taught me to say, '*Perdóneme, por favor.*'"[13]

Buzzer Louis spoke to Lieutenant Chuck. "Do you need us to come there and help, *teniente*?"

---

13. "Excuse me, please"

It was *Capitán Paloma* who answered Buzzer's question. "Yes, please, *señor*." She continued, showing that her *Inglés* was not bad. Not bad at all. "This *Carlos* is a mean motor scooter," she continued, using an expression she had surely picked up from a Hollywood movie. "I remember four years ago when you and *El Señor* Cincinnati trapped him at a wine tasting and tango contest at our Sheraton Hotel, no? What is important, Mr. Louis, is that the two of you know more about *Carlos* the Puma than anyone else does."

"We need your help," *teniente* Chuck jumped in. "Will you come and assist?"

The *capitán* quickly added, "I can arrange for first-class airline tickets tomorrow morning if that is not too soon. From San Antonio in Texas, no?"

"First, yes, we will come," Buzzer said. "And please call me just plain Buzzer. We won't need tickets, though. Cincinnati is a fine pilot. He owns a beautiful twin fanjet Sabreliner with a long-distance pack. We can fly down in his jet faster and more comfortably than taking an airline flight. Dusty is learning to fly. She can help him."

"The pig dances *and* flies his own jet airplane?" Chuck was obviously surprised. "*¡Ay, ya, ya! Me hace reír.*[14] That makes me laugh. Excuse me. I am not being polite, just-plain-Buzzer."

Buzzer Louis laughed at the new name Chuck had just given him. "That's fine, Chuck. *No hay problema.*[15] Right now Cincinnati and my sister Dusty Louise are poring over

---

14. *¡Ay, ya, ya!* is a Hispanic exclamation. *Me hace reír* means 'Makes me laugh.'
15. No problem.

charts and maps. They're looking for a safe, fast route from here at the Hill Country Intergalactic Airport to Buenos Aires. From HCIA to EZE.[16] As soon as we have that figured out, I'll call you back. How's that?"

"Most excellent, just plain Buzzer," Chuck said. "Right now, we should exchange mobile phone numbers. ¿*Verdad?*"[17]

* * *

*In the Dining Room*

While Buzzer Louis and the Argentinean captain and lieutenant were exchanging cell and satellite phone numbers, Dusty and Cincinnati were hard at work at the dining room table. Dr. Buford and Bogart-BOGART were standing by, in case the two flyers needed help. Or some extra wisdom from Dr. Buford's very smart brother.

Dusty was speaking to Cincinnati. "According to the Great Circle Mapper here on the Internet, Cincinnati, it's a bit more than five thousand miles from here to *Buenos Aires*.

So we ought to be able to make just one stop along the way. Even with your long-distance pack, that's a little farther than you can fly without stopping at all, isn't it?"

"Too far without a stop, Dusty," Cincinnati said. "Looks like about ten to eleven hours flying time. Let's see if we can find a good stopping place about halfway there. Say about twenty-five hundred miles from here. That's 4,000 kilometers."

---

16. HCIA and EZE are abbreviated designations for the two airports.
17. "Right?"

"How about this one, Cincinnati?" Dusty Louise pointed to an airport symbol near the west coast of South America. "It's called *Cuzco, Perú*. Looks like it's about halfway to me. What do you think?"

Cincinnati punched up a few keys on his now recharged laptop. He studied the screen for a minute. "Nope, Dusty. Won't work. Too high."

"Do you mean they charge too much to land there?" she asked.

He grinned at this chance to teach Dusty another big lesson about flying.

Dusty looked perplexed. She clearly didn't understand why landing at Cuzco was not a good idea. But she didn't want to look dumb, so she just stared at the map on the table.

And she looked dumb anyway.

"Here's the deal," Cincinnati spoke softly so as not to embarrass her. "The air is just too thin that high up. My plane is heavy. To get enough 'lift' to land safely, we would have to be going too fast for a safe landing. And our take-off might take more runway than this airport's got. It's a matter of air rushing over the wings holding them up. It makes low air pressure over the wing. That lifts us up and keeps us in the air. So we need more air than we can get at ten thousand feet. Got it?"

"*Sí, sí, mi amigo piloto. Yo entiendo bien. Gracias.*"[18] Dusty slipped into the Spanish she was teaching Cincinnati. It was her way of showing that, just like he knew about high alti-

---

18. "Yes, yes my pilot friend. I understand well. Thanks."

tude landings and takeoffs—which she didn't—she knew something he didn't.

Bogart-BOGART was peeping over the tabletop at the maps and charts. "Why not land somewhere right near the Pacific coast?" he asked. "Seems like almost any airport along here . . ." he pointed to where the coastlines of *Colombia* and *Ecuador* and *Perú* all met the ocean . . . "ought to be close to sea level. Give you plenty of thick air, for sure."

"Good thinking, Bogart-BOGART," Dusty said. Looking at the map again, she said to Cincinnati, "How about *Guayaquil* in *Ecuador*? Right here." She pointed.

Again Cincinnati punched up his laptop and stared at the screen.

He smiled. "Perfect, Dusty. *Guayaquil* is almost exactly halfway. It's twenty-five hundred miles from here, and then another twenty-six hundred miles from *Guayaquil* to *Buenos Aires*. Almost perfect. And guess what?"

"It's barely above sea level?" the very smart Labrador retriever guessed.

"Right-o, my very smart friend. Only nineteen feet—six meters—above sea level. And the runway's more than nine thousand feet long. Way more than we'll ever need. So let's plug it in!" Cincinnati said with some pleasure. "We've got our halfway stop."

"What halfway stop?" Luigi had just wandered up. Of course, he had another of his endless questions.

"Halfway to where?" It was the ever-curious Luisa this time, looking for a tidbit of information to get excited about, don't you know?

Dusty looked at the twins. *"En treinta minutos, gemelitos."* [19]

"When Buzzer gets off the phone and back in here, we'll tell you *todas las noticias,"* [20] Dusty said.

*Do you think Socks will let Buzzer and his gang will go to* Buenos Aires *to help the captain and lieutenant and the Argentinean police track down* Carlos *the Puma? Do you think* Cincinnati's *right that* Carlos *the Puma is very smart and will get to* Buenos Aires *in five days? Or less? Are there going to be problems landing at* Guayaquil *near the Pacific Ocean in* Ecuador? *When do you think* los cuatro gatos tejanos [21] *and Cincinnati will really be able to leave? And how long will it take them to get to where they're going? Can Cincinnati's plane go over the really high Andes Mountains in South America?*

---

19. "In thirty minutes, little twins."
20. All the news
21. The four Texan cats

# Aprendamos a Hablar en Español
by Dusty Louise

Now that you know *los colores bien*, how about the *calendario*? *¿Entiendes los días de la semana? ¿Los meses del año?* Here's some help for you. *Es fácil. ¿Verdad?*[22]

## CALENDAR

| In English | In Spanish | Say It Like This |
|---|---|---|
| Days | *Días* | DEE-ahs |
| Monday | *Lunes* | LOO-nehs |
| Tuesday | *Martes* | MAHR-tehs |
| Wednesday | *Miércoles* | Mee-AIR-coh-lehs |
| Thursday | *Jueves* | WHAY-vehs |
| Friday | *Viernes* | Vee-AIR-nehs |
| Saturday | *Sábado* | SAH-bah-doh |
| Sunday | *Domingo* | Doh-MEEN-goh |
| Months | *Meses* | MAY-sehs |
| January | *Enero* | Ay-NAIR-oh |
| February | *Febrero* | Feh-BRER-oh |
| March | *Marzo* | MAHR-szoh |
| April | *Abril* | Ah-BREEL |
| May | *Mayo* | MY-oh |
| June | *Junio* | HOO-nyo |
| July | *Julio* | HOOL-yo |
| August | *Agosto* | Ah-GHOST-oh |
| September | *Septiembre* | Sep-tee-IHM-breh |
| October | *Octubre* | Ock-TOO-breh |
| November | *Noviembre* | Noh-vee-IHM-breh |
| December | *Diciembre* | Dee-see-IHM-breh |
| Weeks | *Semanas* | See-MAH-nahs |
| Years | *Años* | AHN-yohs |

---

22. Now that you know your colors well, how about the calendar? Do you know the days of the week? The months of the year? It's easy, right?

# Part Two

## On the Road. Again.

"Catching *Carlos* last time almost was the end of my friend Buzzer Louis. He nearly drowned in the big fountain in front of the Sheraton in *Buenos Aires*, and he still won't talk about it.

This time we'll have to be more careful."

—Cincinnati the dancing pig

# * Chapter 4 *
## *Los Ayudantes Están en el Avión*[1]

*Midnight. on the Tarmac at HCIA*

Dusty Louise had changed frequencies and announced to the tower at HCIA that the little Sabreliner was ready to go. "Hill Country tower, this is Sabreliner seven-zero-niner-niner-alpha. We're ready to take off bound for *Buenos Aires*. Halfway stop at *Simón Bolívar* airport in *Guayaquil*."

It was midnight. The lights on runway three lit up, brightening the 6,000-foot concrete strip.

*Los cuatro gatos tejanos y el cerdo bailarín*[2] had slept five or six hours after Socks gave the "okay" to head to *Buenos Aires*. Socks had even wired 25,000 Argentinean *pesos* to the American Express office in downtown *Buenos Aires* to cover expenses. She would bill Argentina and maybe Brazil for the real costs.

"Sabreliner niner-niner-alpha. You are cleared for takeoff on runway three. Leaving two thousand feet. . . contact San

---

1. The Helpers are in the Airplane.
2. The four Texan cats and the dancing pig.

Antonio departure on frequency one three two point seven. Safe trip. *¡Vaya con Dios, señorita!*"[3]

Dusty rolled to the center of runway three. She lined up on the white dashes down the middle and lowered flaps to fifteen degrees. Spooled up the twin fanjets to ninety-five percent power. At a hooves-up sign from Cincinnati, she took her feet off the brakes and set the little jet screaming down the runway into the wind and up into the Hill Country sky.

"On our way," Cincinnati said, smiling at Dusty's near perfect takeoff. She's learning fast, he thought. Gears up at 3,600 feet. *Muy bien.*[4]

Cincinnati flipped on the intercom and spoke to Buzzer Louis, Luigi Panettone Giaccomazza and Luisa Manicotti Giaccomazza in the cabin behind the cockpit.

"It's just past midnight, *amigos.*[5] We'll be cruising at

---

3. "Go with God, Miss."
4. Very good.
5. friends

about 450 knots—a little more than 500 miles per hour. That'll put us in *Guayaquil* at the *Simón Bolívar* airport to refuel at about five in the morning, Hill Country time. Both *The Flying Pig Machine* and ourselves. We'll grab some breakfast there. So sit back and relax. Sleep if you can. It's going to be a long day." Cincinnati turned off the intercom.

He glanced over at Dusty, who was studying the instrument cluster in front of her.

As the little Sabreliner climbed through five thousand feet, Cincinnati said, "Dusty, turn to 147 degrees, please. Maintain that heading. Let's take her up to 33,000 feet. When we get there, level off and reduce power to about eighty percent. Just enough to hold our speed at about 450 knots."

Meanwhile, back in the cabin, there would likely be no sleep for Buzzer for a while. Luigi and Luisa had begun playing their favorite airplane game. They called it "jumpseat." The tiny orange tabbies would get up on the top of a seat back. Then, like frogs, they would leap to the top of the next seat. Around and around the cabin they went, calling out "Ribbit" with each leap.

The game kept them busy as long as the air outside the little jet was calm. If they ran into turbulence, though, they'd have to stop and buckle up. Of course.

*The Flying Pig Machine* climbed steadily to cruising altitude. As Dusty Louise leveled the little jet and pulled back on the throttles, Luigi and Luisa began to tire of their first round of jumpseat. So together they climbed onto Buzzer's lap, one to each knee. "Tell us a story, Buzzer. Pleeeze!" Luigi begged.

Luisa joined in quickly. "Yes, Buzz. Tell us about when you and Cincinnati captured *Carlos* the Puma last time. We've forgotten that story already."

Luigi chimed in, "Right, Buzzer. Can't remember a thing about it. Tell us again. It might be important when we try to capture him this time."

"Oh, it will be important, Luigi," Luisa said quickly. "Very important. Tell us again, Buzzy." Luisa cocked her head and batted her eyelashes at her big brother. She knew that made her look cute. And she knew Buzzer couldn't resist her and Luigi when they were cute, which, these days, was most of the time.

With *The Flying Pig Machine* on autopilot, and Dusty Louise in the cockpit watching after things, Cincinnati walked back into the cabin. "What are you two begging for this time?" he asked.

Buzzer answered, "They want me to tell them about four years ago, when you and I trapped *Carlos* the Puma the first time. Cincinnati, you know I don't much like to tell that story."

Buzzer looked at the dancing pig, whose forehead was wrinkled in a frown. Cincinnati knew the problem. Buzzer had almost drowned back then. Retelling the story always made him feel bad. The dancing pig took the hint.

"Why don't I tell you the story? I was there, too. Besides, I think Buzzer needs to go up into the cockpit and talk to Dusty. Right, *compadre*?"[6]

Buzzer Louis stood and made his way up to the cockpit.

---

6. Literally, the father of one's godchild. Figuratively, 'old friend.'

He would talk with his sister Dusty Louise while Cincinnati told the wide-awake twins the story of the first capture of *Carlos* the Puma.

First, though, Cincinnati went to the little galley and got himself a big cup of coffee. He gave the twins each a box of juice, and the three of them settled in for a story.

* * *

*Brasil. On the Amazon River. Near Manaus.*

The thirty-nine foot river trawler *Meteoro*[7] chugged slowly in the darkness, headed for the Atlantic Ocean at the mouth of the Amazon River. The *Meteoro* was running in the dark. It had come a day and a night from *Boa Vista* on a northern tributary, almost all the way from the borders with *Venezuela* and *Guyana*.

The trawler's only passenger was a big cat. A dangerous cat: the international terrorist, *Carlos* the Puma, who had paid the ship's captain a year's worth of fares to take him from *Boa Vista* to the Atlantic Ocean. A long trip for sure, but it took him from the prison, where he'd been held for almost four years, halfway to *Buenos Aires*.

Nobody else was allowed on the *Meteoro*. Just *Carlos* and *Capitán Ramos*. No crew. Not even any real freight. Just some empty crates stacked on the deck to look as though they were being shipped. *Carlos* did allow the captain to

---

7. Meteor

pick up mail along the way to take to *São Paulo*. That was because the *Meteoro* always did the mail run. Any change in that habit might cause suspicion. At every mail stop, the big cat slipped below deck to hide in the captain's quarters.

They had come far enough that the Amazon was now wide. So wide the big cat couldn't see either shore, but a vast expanse of water in all directions, full of crocs and piranhas. As they chugged along, *Carlos* smiled to himself. He would go to Argentina.

*Capitán Ramos*

He would find the cat and the pig who had trapped him in *Buenos Aires* four years before. And he would even the score.

*Carlos* wasn't sure what he would do to Buzzer Louis and Cincinnati the dancing pig. But he knew it would be a slow and painful process. He was, after all, a master terrorist. A "mean motor scooter" he snickered to himself, finding the term pretty funny.

"They will pay. They will pay." Suddenly he realized he was talking out loud.

Looking down from his perch on the platform bridge behind the boat's big wheel, the captain asked *Carlos*, "Were you talking to me?"

*Carlos* the Puma snarled. "If I'm talking to you, *Ramos*, your ears will burn. You'll know when I want to talk to you, *lunático peludo.*[8] Who I'm talking to, *capitán, no es asunto tuyo.*[9] You just get me to the ocean by tomorrow. *¡Y cierra la boca!*"[10]

Suddenly lights appeared on the river, far in front of the trawler. "Get below," *Capitán Ramos* warned. "It's a fast-moving boat. Could be the authorities."

*Carlos* didn't like being told what to do, but he knew *Ramos* was right. It was time to disappear below decks until the danger of being discovered had passed.

Quietly, *Carlos* slipped below. The captain shut down his diesel engine and let the trawler drift with the current. Maybe the other boat wouldn't even see them.

* * *

*At 33,000 feet over Central America. In The Flying Pig Machine*

Luigi and Luisa were still wide-awake. They were waiting for Cincinnati to tell them about capturing *Carlos*. They sucked their apple juice through tiny straws and peeped out the window. The night was clear. They saw a coastline pass under the little jet, and then saw the lights of a big city.

"Where are we, Cincinnati?" Luisa asked, pointing to the lights below.

"That should be *Guatemala City*, Luisa, in Central America. We just crossed over *Mérida* on the Mexican Yucatán. Remember *Mérida*, boys and girls?" He smiled.

"That's where we captured Fred-X." Luigi shouted. "The first time."

---

8. shaggy lunatic
9. is none of your business, captain
10. "And shut your mouth!"

"Maybe we could get *Carlos* the Puma to come there, too," Luisa offered. "It's a good place to catch bad guys, for sure."

Luigi sat up and looked at Cincinnati. *"Pero primero, cerdo bailarín, díganos el cuento de usted y Buzzer con Carlos el Puma en Buenos Aires, por favor, señor."* [11]

Startled, Luigi abruptly stopped talking. Turning to Luisa, he shrugged as if to ask, "What just happened?"

Luisa smiled and slowly clapped her front paws. "Yes, Luigi," she said slowly, "you just spoke to Cincinnati in perfect Spanish. *Buen trabajo, hermanito.*[12] Dusty won't be the only almighty translator by the time this trip's over."

The thought of getting one-up on Dusty caused the kittens to laugh out loud.

Cincinnati sat down and started the story the twins wanted to hear. Of course they had heard it many times before, so before he got much past "Once upon a time, four years ago," both kittens were yawning and blinking. Within a minute both were snoozing away, leaning against one another.

Cincinnati reached down and fastened a seat belt around the two of them. He went back to the cockpit to check on their progress as they flew southeast at 33,000 feet, and 500 miles per hour.

*Do you think the boat that appeared on the Amazon River will see the* Meteoro *and discover the escaped* Carlos *the Puma? What about the twins' story? Will they ever get to hear it again? How about Dusty? It's a long way to* Buenos Aires. *Our travelers aren't even to* Guayaquil *yet. Will Dusty be able to stay awake*

---

11. "But first, dancing pig, tell us the story of you and Buzzer with Carlos the Puma in Buenos Aires, please, sir."
12. Good work, little brother.

all the way? And what of Buzzer Louis? Will he ever be able to talk about capturing Carlos *in* Buenos Aires *without feeling bad?*

# Aprendamos a Hablar en Español
## by Dusty Louise

Now that you know your way around the calendar, *aprendamos algunas palabras y frases útiles.*[13]

## PALABRAS Y FRASES ÚTILES

| In English | In Spanish | Say It Like This |
|---|---|---|
| Thank you | Gracias | GRAH-see-ahs |
| You're welcome | De nada | Day NAH-dah |
| (greeting) Hello | Hola | OH-lah |
| (answering phone) Hello | Pronto or Listo | PROHN-toh, LEESZ-toh |
| Goodbye | Adiós | Ah-dee-OHS |
| Good/well | Bien | Bee-IHN |
| Very good | Muy bien | MOO-ee bee-IHN |
| Please | Por favor | POHR fah-VOHR |
| At your service | A sus órdenes | Ah soosz OHR-dehn-ehs |
| I want to introduce you to | Quiero presentarle a | Kee-AIR-oh pray-sihn-TAHR-leh ah |
| Sir | Señor | Seen-YOHR |
| Ma'am | Señora | Seen-YOHR-ah |
| Miss | Señorita | Seen-yohr-EE-tah |

---

13. We're going to learn some useful words and phrases.

| What time is it? | ¿Qué hora es? | Kay OHRAH ess |
| Where are we going? | ¿A dónde vamos? | Ah DOHN-day VAH-mos |
| Ready? | ¿Listo? | LEE-stoh |
| Let's go! | ¡Vámonos! | VAH-moh-nohs |
| Okay, good, sure | Bueno | BWAIN-oh |
| More slowly | Más despacio | MAHS deh-SPAH-see-oh |
| Faster | Más rápido | MAHS RAH-pee-doh |
| How's it going? | ¿Qué tal? | Kay TAHL |
| Maybe, perhaps | Tal vez | Tahl VASZ |
| Do you speak English? | ¿Habla usted Inglés? | AH-blah oo-STED een-GLASZ |
| I do not speak Spanish well. | No hablo Español bien. | Noh AH-bloh es-pahn-YOLL bee-IHN |
| Where is a telephone? | ¿Dónde está un teléfono? | DOAN-deh ess-TAH oon teh-LAY-foh-noh |
| How much does it cost? | ¿Cuánto cuesta? | KWAHN-toh KWAY-stah |
| Where is the bathroom? | ¿Dónde está el cuarto de baño? | DOAN-day ess-TAH el KWAHR-toh day BAHN-yoh |
| I'm sorry. | Lo siento. | Loh see-IHN-toh |
| Excuse me, pardon me | Perdóneme | Pair-DOHN-ah-may |
| That's very pretty. | Eso es muy lindo. | AY-soh ess MOO-ey LEEN-doh. |
| No, thank you. | No, gracias. | NOH GRAH-see-ahs |
| I'm very hungry. | Tengo mucha hambre. | TAHN-goh MOO-chah AHM-bray |

# * Chapter 5 *

## *El Puma Grande Está en el Río. Los Gatos Pequeños y el Cerdo Están en el Cielo.*[1]

*Capitán Ramos* peered out from behind a plywood partition on the rear deck of the *Meteoro*. He watched the lights of the distant but fast-moving boat, and just let his boat float quietly with the current.

Now the lights were approaching, and he crossed his fingers that those in the other boat wouldn't see him. *Ramos* wasn't sure about his passenger—the cat wouldn't even tell him his name—but *Ramos* was fairly sure the big puma was running from something. Or to something. *Ramos* didn't want trouble, but he did want all the money the cat would pay him. So far he'd gotten half. The other half was waiting at their destination.

Now he could hear the approaching boat. As *Ramos*

---

1. The Big Puma is on the River. The Little Cats and a Pig are in the Sky.

watched, the running lights coming up the river began to slow. He heard the engine slow as well, and then he saw the lights turning toward him. It was clear they had seen the *Meteoro*.

How will I explain why I've got my running lights off? he wondered. He reached for a long curved knife on a shelf by the *Meteoro*'s steering wheel and stuck it in his right boot. Just in case.

All at once a thought struck him. Just as the other boat pulled alongside, he lifted the cover over his engine, propped it open and grabbed a flashlight. He noted the boat was a fast speedboat. Cigarette boats, they were called, and they were mostly used for running drugs at night. This one looked innocent enough, though. *Ramos* leaned over his motor, pretending he was having engine trouble.

"Everything all right here?" a short man on the other boat shouted. "You need help?"

*Ramos* waved at the man. "*No, gracias,*" he said. "*Todo está bien, señor.*"[2] With that, he turned the key and the well-maintained diesel started right up. *Ramos* flipped on the running lights.

"*Está bien ahora. ¡Gracias también, señor!*"[3] *Ramos* assured the man in the other boat.

Thinking it best to get away, *Ramos* put his trawler in gear and moved slowly away from the cigarette boat, waving farewell as he increased his speed.

Just then, *Carlos* the Puma leaped up onto the deck and threw a glass jar of diesel fuel with a lighted rag for a fuse into the other boat. It was a classic Molotov cocktail, and it

---

2. "No, thank you. Everything is fine, sir."
3. "It's fine now. Thanks again, sir."

exploded with a flash. Instantly, fire spread throughout the cigarette boat.

It was going to burn, and sink. No doubt about it.

*Carlos* shouted, "*Ramos*, get this boat moving. We have to get away from here. *¡Lo más pronto posible, capitán!*"[4]

*Ramos* was furious. Why had that cat decided to sink the cigarette boat?

Fearing what the big cat might do next, *Ramos* shoved the throttle wide open. The trawler reared its bow and plowed straight down the Amazon, away from the burning hulk in the water. They left a wake that caused the fire on the cigarette boat to bob up and down crazily.

*Ramos* looked straight ahead. He kept his back to the big cat. But he could hear the puma gulping air, as if sinking a boat with a firebomb was exciting to him.

Also, he could smell the big puma. It was as if burning the other boat caused the big cat to give off a peculiar, though not unpleasant, smell.

Odd.

Now *Ramos* was sure about his passenger: sure he wanted to get to the Atlantic as quickly as possible. He wanted to collect the other half of his money and be rid of this crazy big cat for good.

\* \* \*

*Over the Pacific Ocean. Off the coast of Panamá.*

The time was 3:05 A.M. on the digital clock on the bulk-

---

4. As fast as possible, captain!

head separating the main cabin from the galley. That is, 3:05 A.M. Hill Country time.

The little Sabreliner had covered almost 1,500 miles, and it was now over the Pacific Ocean. The west coast of *Panamá* was clearly visible on the distant horizon far outside the left-hand windows—or the "port" side, as Cincinnati referred to "left."

Luigi and Luisa had slept less than an hour and a half, and now they were back at a new game of jumpseat. They leapt around the little jet's cabin, "ribbit-ing" with every leap, and having a very good time, for sure.

Cincinnati the dancing pig wandered back into the cabin from the cockpit. He held up his front legs as a sign for the twins to stop jumping, at least for a minute.

"We're going to be over water for the next hour or so before we start our descent into *Simón Bolívar* airport in *Guayaquil*," he said to Buzzer and the twins. "Ought to be a very smooth ride."

"We want our story," Luigi piped up.

"Right," Luisa added. "You never told us the story, Cincinnati."

Cincinnati winked at Buzzer. "Yes, I did, Luisa. I guess the two of you just slept through it."

"No we didn't. You didn't tell us," Luigi said.

"Well, I guess we have time for it before we start down to refuel," the dancing pig said. "Buzzer, you want to go visit with Dusty Louise again?"

Buzzer didn't answer. He just stood up and moved forward. He stopped in the galley for a glass of milk, then stepped into the cockpit and closed the door behind him.

"Okay, boys and girls," Cincinnati began. "Here's the story of the first time we captured *Carlos* the Puma. It all happened at the Sheraton Hotel in *Buenos Aires* four years ago. But you have to promise me you'll stay awake. Okay?"

"We promise," Luisa said, batting her lashes and cocking her head.

Luigi closed his eyes and began a loud fake snoring, pretending he was already asleep. But he couldn't keep from laughing. He popped open his eyes suddenly with a big grin, stood up and saluted Cincinnati as if the dancing pig were a general. "Right, sir! Wide-awake. And waiting for your story."

"*Bien, gemelos pequeños. Esta es la historia de* Buzzer Louis, Cincinnati *el cerdo bailarín, y Carlos en Argentina.*[5]

"It was four years ago. *Carlos* the Puma had just brought down the fifty-third Italian government since World War II. Cleverly, he had poisoned more than a dozen members of the Socialist party. Sure, all the deaths were found to be 'natural causes.' But Buzzer and I, we knew. So did worldwide law enforcement. We clearly saw the paw prints of *Carlos* all over the death certificates. He had made fools of the carabinieri—the Italian national police.

"They weren't the first to be fooled by *Carlos*, for sure. Not at all. You could toss in Scotland Yard, Interpol, the Duxieme, the F.B.I.—even the Stasi and the KGB. *Carlos*

---

5. "Okay, little twins. Here is the story of Buzzer Louis, Cincinnati the dancing pig, and Carlos in Argentina."

was simply the best—or maybe the worst—international saboteur ever."

"What happened at the Sheraton Hotel?" Luisa was definitely catching the impatience of her big sister, Dusty Louise.

Cincinnati continued, "Buzzer and I had tracked him from *Fiumicino*, the big airport near Rome, to *Buenos Aires*. Interpol had insisted that *Carlos* used Argentina for his base. We saw him on a customs video, entering Argentina posing as a Chinese shoe salesman."

"How did you catch him?" Now Luigi was interrupting with questions.

"Like every high-living bad guy," Cincinnati went on, "*Carlos* had his weaknesses. In his case, he was smitten with great wine. And he loved dancing with beautiful women. So Buzzer and I dreamed up an international wine-tasting and tango contest. Entries were invited from all over Argentina. All of South America, actually.

"We knew he would enter. Sure enough, on a night not much different from this one, there he was. Half of couple number fifty-seven in the tango contest. His partner was a stunning young Brazilian girl, from *Ipanema*.[6] Poetic, no?"

"I guess so," Luigi said, not sure what the dancing pig meant by 'poetic.'

"But how did Buzzer nearly die?" asked Luisa, cutting to the chase.

"Well, Buzzer got us appointed head judges of the tango contest. It was held in a big ballroom on the twenty-third floor of the Sheraton Hotel. Buzzer's job was to ferret out

---

6. *Ipanema* is a beach in *Río de Janeiro* in Brazil. It's a Portuguese word.

*Carlos* and chase him off the balcony outside the ballroom. I was waiting down below with the fire department. And the police. And a big net. We could catch *Carlos* the Puma and wrap him up. Once and for all."

"What went wrong?" Luisa asked, still pressing for a finish to the story.

"Nothing really went wrong, Luisa. Be patient. We're almost done," Cincinnati said.

"Buzzer patiently waited by the double glass balcony doors until *Carlos* and the girl from *Ipanema* came by during the tango contest. When they got near the doors, Buzzer rushed at them. *Carlos* recognized him. He ran through the doors onto the balcony. Never slowing down, he jumped into the night air, right off that balcony. Just as we planned for him to do.

"Buzzer was right behind him," Cincinnati went on. "He was starting to slow down so as not to go over the edge himself. Then the unexpected happened. The girl from *Ipanema* tossed a wine glass at Buzzer. He hopped to miss the broken glass. As he slid sideways, he lost his balance and went over the edge of the balcony, only seconds behind *Carlos*.

"It was a long way to the ground, and there was only one net ready."

"Couldn't you catch both of them in the net?" Luisa asked.

"Not really. *Carlos* fell first, and Buzzer was only about halfway down when the net snapped around the puma. Buzzer could see that there was no net to catch him, so, to try and slow his fall, he spread out his arms and legs as if he were a cat-skin rug. I saw what he was doing, so I grabbed two flashlights from *la policía.*ʹ Like a signalman, I guided him to the big fountain in front of the Sheraton. He hit with a mighty splash. A perfect cannonball, I've often kidded him.

"But it wasn't funny that night. Buzzer was knocked out cold when he hit the water. He almost drowned. Oh, he had a few bruises, but the water's what almost got him. I pulled him from the fountain and gave him mouth-to-mouth resuscitation."

Cincinnati went on, "We didn't think he was going to make it. But just as we were about to give up, he spit out a mouthful of water, and began breathing again."

"Yay! Bravo!" Luigi and Luisa were clapping and jumping up and down.

"Do you know what Buzzer's first words were after

---

7. the police

that?" Cincinnati asked. Without waiting for an answer, he went on, "He said, 'Did we get *Carlos?*' Your big brother is a genuine hero, kids."

"Wow, Buzzer really is a hero!" Luigi stood and saluted. But he stood so fast that he toppled over backward.

Luisa and Cincinnati laughed as Cincinnati added, "*Sí, Luigi, Buzzer es un héroe. En seis continentes. Una leyenda, cierto.*[8] Never forget what a special big brother you have."

Dusty Louise stuck her head out the cockpit door. "Cincinnati, the autopilot's beeping. I think it's almost time to begin our descent into *Simón Bolívar en Guayaquil,*"[9] she said.

"Back to the cockpit for me," Cincinnati said as he turned and started forward.

Buzzer exited the cockpit to make room for Cincinnati. As they passed in the aisle, Luisa had a question for her big brother. "What's a *Simón Bolívar?*" she asked.

Buzzer sat down. "*Simón Bolívar* is a big hero in South America," he said. "He helped many countries win their independence from *Spain* about two hundred years ago. In fact, at one time or another, he was president of *Colombia, Venezuela, Bolivia,* and *Perú.* How's that for a hero?"

"We already have a hero," Luigi said.

"But we're not telling who he is," Luisa added with a smile.

"Tell us something strange about *Simón Bolívar,* Buzzer," Luigi said. He liked to hear strange facts. He often said he would write a book about strange little facts some day.

"Well, Luigi, he may have had the longest name in history," Buzzer said.

---

8. "Yes, Luigi, Buzzer is a hero. On six continents. A legend, in fact."
9. *Simón Bolívar* airport in *Guayaquil, Ecuador*

"Longer than 'Luigi Panettone Giaccomazza?'" Luisa asked.

"Much longer," Buzzer said.

"What was it?" the twins spoke in unison.

"Let me be sure about it," Buzzer said, and he opened his laptop and turned it on. He typed a few keystrokes into Google®.

"Here it is," Buzzer said. "*Simón José Antonio de la Santísima Trinidad de Bolívar y Palacios Blanco. How's that for a name?*" Buzzer smiled.

"Holy *frijoles!*"[10] Luigi said. "I'm going to have an airport named for me one day."

Just then Cincinnati spoke over the intercom. "Buckle up, *amigos*. We're about a hundred miles out from *Guayaquil* and beginning our descent. We'll be on the ground in fifteen minutes, at 5:05 A.M. Hill Country time."

As Cincinnati spooled down the two engines, he slowed the little jet and pointed its nose downward. They were about to land in *Ecuador*.

*Why do you think* Carlos *firebombed the cigarette boat on the Amazon River? What do you think will happen when the puma and* Capitán Ramos *get to the Atlantic Ocean? Will* Ramos *get the rest of his money? Will he turn* Carlos *in to the authorities? Will* los cuatro gatos tejanos y su amigo el cerdo bailarín[11] *be able to get breakfast at the* Simón Bolívar *airport in* Guayaquil, Ecuador? *Will there be a Chevron truck to fill up the tanks of* The Flying Pig Machine?

---

10. "Holy beans!"
11. the four Texan cats and their friend the dancing pig

# Aprendamos a Hablar en Español
## by Dusty Louise

*Ahora vamos a aprender acerca del tiempo. Es importante entender las palabras y frases significativas acerca del tiempo.[12]*

## EL TIEMPO

| In English | In Spanish | Say It Like This |
|---|---|---|
| Weather | Tiempo | Tee-IHM-poh |
| Climate | El clima | Ehl CLEE-mah |
| It is hot | Hace calor | AH-say cah-LOHR |
| It is cold | Hace frío | AH-say FREE-oh |
| It is windy | Hay viento | EYE vee-IHN-toh |
| Rain | Lluvia | YOU-vee-ah |
| It is raining | Está lloviendo | Ess-TAH yoh-vee-IHN-doh |
| Rainy | Lluvioso | You-vee-OH-soh |
| Snow | Nieve | Nee-AY-vee |
| Clouds | Nubes | NOO-behsz |
| Storm | Tormenta | Tohr-MEHN-tah |
| Thunder | Trueno | Troo-AY-noh |
| Lightning | Relámpago | Ray-LAHM-pah-goh |
| Hail | Granizo | Grah-NEE-zoh |
| Temperature | Temperatura | Tehm-pair-ah-TOO-rah |
| Sun | El sol | Ehl SOHL |
| Sunlight | Luz del sol | Looz del SOHL |
| Moon | La luna | Lah-LOO-nah |
| Moonlight | Luz de la luna | LOOSZ deh-lah LOO-nah |

---

12. Now we're going to learn about the weather. It's important to understand significant words and phrases about the weather.

# * Chapter 6 *
## *El Avión Acaba de Aterrizar.*
## *El Bote Atracó También.*[1]

*Over the Pacific. Just off the Coast of Ecuador.*

"*Simón Bolívar* tower, this is Sabreliner seven-zero-niner-niner-alpha, forty miles to your northwest, proceeding direct, requesting clearance to land and refuel." Dusty Louise was getting really good at talking to airport towers. All over the world.

"Sabreliner niner-niner-alpha, this is *Simón Bolívar* tower. Plan to enter left base for runway three. There is no other traffic in the area, miss. Taxi to your right and park on the apron outside the passenger loading area. We'll send a Shell truck with Jet A. Welcome to *Guayaquil*, Miss. Will you need to deplane?"

"*Sí, sí, señor, por favor. Necesitamos algo de desayuna para cuatro gatos tejanos y un cerdo bailarín.*"[2]

---

1. The plane just landed. The boat landed, too.
2. "Yes, yes, sir. We need some breakfast for four Texan cats and a dancing pig."

"Excellent, Miss. I'll send a courtesy vehicle to bring you and your passengers to the terminal. As you know, you may not leave the terminal without passing through customs. But for breakfast, *no es necesario*.[3] Wind is from the northeast at nine knots steady. Temperature is twenty-four degrees Celsius."

"*Gracias, señor*," Dusty replied. "*Muchas gracias*."

"*De nada, señorita. Con mucho gusto*,"[4] the voice from the tower answered.

Soon after, as the conversation with the tower ended, Cincinnati made a sharp left turn. He lowered the little jet's flaps some more and engaged the speed brakes. As *The Flying Pig Machine* floated gently over the end of the runway, he cut back the power and dropped like a feather onto runway three. With a tiny screech, the plane's tires were on the ground. Thrusters reversed and brakes on, the little jet slowed quickly.

Dusty took the controls to taxi to the spot outside the passenger loading area, where the Shell truck would refill the Sabreliner's tanks for the remaining 2,600 miles—or 4,200 kilometers—to *Buenos Aires*. Meanwhile, the four cats and Cincinnati refilled their own tanks with some breakfast.

✳ ✳ ✳

———
3. it's not necessary
4. "You're welcome, Miss. It's my pleasure"

# * El Avión Acaba de Aterrizar *

*En El Bote Meteoro. En El Río Amazonas.*[5]

*"El bote se está acercando el puerto de Marañón, Señor Puma,"*[6] Capitán *Ramos* shouted down the stairwell leading below decks. *"Tengo mucho correo para entregar aquí."*[7] He had been told to speak to the big cat only in Spanish. This was *Carlos'* rule.

*Ramos* usually stopped at towns and villages along the north bank of the big river on his trips into the Amazon basin—upriver. Then he stopped along the south bank on his return to the Atlantic. Round trips took him ten days. This stop at *Marañón* was as regular as sunrise and sunset for the captain. But he worried about what that crazy big cat might do before they slipped away and headed on downriver.

More than ever, he was anxious to get the big—and clearly troubled—puma off his boat. And collect the other half of his money. Just to be safe, he wanted to take the first half into the village and wire it from a bank to his account in *Río de Janeiro*. This was in case the big cat got any ideas about sinking the *Meteoro*, like he had sunk the cigarette boat a few hours before, and then making off with *Ramos'* cash.

Right after killing him.

But getting away from the boat and leaving the big puma unwatched? *Ramos* was sure that would be a mistake. He just couldn't risk it.

*Marañón* was one of the larger stops on *Ramos'* regular run. Instead of the typical wooden docks built out into the river, this stop had real boat slips. *Ramos* always

---

5. On the boat *Meteoro*. On the Amazon River
6. "The boat's landing at the port of *Marañón*, Mister (lion) Puma."
7. "I have a lot of mail to deliver here."

pulled into the center slip, the one closest to the town's main street.

Several dock hands wandered out to pay their respects to the captain. They either worked on the docks, or they just loafed there—*Ramos* was never sure which. If he was going to trust one of them to take his money to a local bank, he'd rather it be a real worker instead of someone who just loafed about all day waiting for another boat to come in.

The *Meteoro* was snugged up against a couple of pilings that held up the dock. Pilings were made from the millions of trees in the rain forest surrounding the town.

As *Ramos* gathered the big bundle of mail for *Marañón*, he saw out of the corner of his eye that the puma was slinking up from below deck. *Carlos* had crept over to one of the pilings. Suddenly he disappeared behind the piling, leaving the deck of the boat completely.

*Ramos* had decided to leave his money on board—not to trust any of the dockhands with it even though he had known some of them for years.

He wanted to just drop off his bundle of mail, pick up any mail headed for *São Paulo*, and get back on the river. The sooner he got that big cat to the Atlantic and got rid of him, the better.

Exchanging mail packets with a local postal worker, *Ramos* called to some of the idlers on the dock to untie the ropes holding the *Meteoro* against the pilings so he could cast off. As he started his diesel engine, he saw the big puma slink back across the deck and down into the cabin below.

*Ramos* turned his thirty-nine foot trawler as it backed out into the current. He shifted into forward gear and opened up the throttle. Running with the current, he was sure he could be at the Atlantic mouth of the Amazon by tomorrow afternoon, which was about another thirty hours. That's what he had promised the big cat, anyway: to get him to the mouth of the Amazon River in three and a half days would mean running much faster than usual.

*Ramos* moved the *Meteoro* out into the current, where they could make the best time. Before they had gone a mile, suddenly there was an ear-splitting explosion behind them. *Ramos* looked back to see shock waves, lumber, pilings and smoke flying straight out from the docks they had just left. At the base of the confusion were red flames shooting skyward.

*Ramos* thought, That crazy big cat has just bombed the docks at *Marañón. ¿Por qué? ¿Está loco? ¿Totalmente?*[8]

As these questions raced through his head, *Ramos* began to smell the same odor he had smelled after the cigarette boat incident. This cat does something *completamente loco y entonces se pone mal oliente. Me confunde,*[9] he said to himself.

*Ramos* pushed his throttle all the way to the stop. He began to think the other half of the money the puma would pay him wasn't worth any more of the big cat's crazy behavior—or his funny smell!

* * *

---

8. Why? Is he crazy? Completely?
9. "does something completely crazy and then he smells bad. It confuses me."

*Al Aeropuerto Simón Bolívar en Guayaquil. Otra Vez.*[10]

Cincinnati wandered into the coffee shop where *los cuatro gatos tejanos* had already ordered their breakfasts. He had stayed behind while *los dos hombres de Shell*[11] refueled *The Flying Pig Machine*. While Cincinnati had never had any serious trouble with refueling, he sensed they were getting closer to *Carlos* the Puma. And he just didn't trust that cat.

"Hi, Cincinnati," Luigi piped up. "We ordered you a big bowl of Cheerios® and a cup of coffee and some orange juice. I hope that's okay with you."

"*Es bueno, gatito,*"[12] Cincinnati responded, glancing at Dusty Louise to be sure his Spanish *era bueno también.*[13]

Luisa joined the conversation. "We were careful not to order any *tocineta o jamón,*[14] Cincinnati," she said. "We thought you might not like that."

Cincinnati laughed. "Those are not my favorite foods, for sure, Luisa. And I'll be sure not to eat any *filete de gato, también, amigos.*"[15]

While they ate their breakfast, Buzzer Louis and Dusty Louise were watching CNN Worldwide on a television set on the wall. Buzzer was having *un gran wafle con las fresas y crema bate.*[16] And Dusty was eating *pan tostado con mantequilla y mermelada de uvas.*[17]

Suddenly, both Buzzer Louis and Dusty Louise jumped

---

10. At Simón Bolívar Airport in Guayaquil. Once Again.
11. the two men from Shell
12. 'That's good, little kitten,'
13. Spanish was good also.
14. bacon or ham
15. cat steak, too, my friends.
16. a big waffle with strawberries and whipped cream
17. toast with butter and grape marmalade

up and pointed to the television. Buzzer shouted, *"¡Silencio. Miren la televisión!"* [18]

A CNN reporter was standing by a smoldering, burning dock in *Marañón, Brasil.* She was recounting how someone had apparently planted a bomb here less than two hours ago, blowing up six boat slips in the process. She said there was no apparent reason yet for the bombing, and no organization had, as yet, taken credit. She went on to say that the bombing followed by two hours another bombing—of a cigarette boat about one hundred kilometers up river.

"Some are speculating that these two acts are linked," the reporter said." "And they may be the work of that infamous international terrorist, *Carlos* the Puma. *Carlos* escaped from a dreadful prison far up-river two days ago. According to Brazilian officials, these two acts bear the trademarks of the big cat. This is Silvia Dematté reporting for CNN from the Amazon River, near *Marañón, Brasil.*"

"What do you think, Buzzer?" Dusty asked. "Are these bombings the work of *Carlos* the Puma?"

"*Sin duda*, Dusty,"[19] Cincinnati jumped in to answer the question. "It's like he's practicing. You know, taking on small targets."

"Exactly," Buzzer said. "Getting ready to do something really big. But he's a little out of practice. He must need to sharpen up his skills again, so he picked a cigarette boat and some slips at a little dock. Oh, yes. It's *Carlos*, all right."

"He's still a long way from *Buenos Aires*, Buzzer. Did you see the map behind that reporter, Silvia? If he's going all the

18. "Quiet! Look at the television!"
19. "Without doubt."

way to the Atlantic Ocean, he has a ways to go still," Luisa said. She had been paying close attention to the CNN report.

"Right," Luigi said, somewhat seriously for the little prankster. He turned to Buzzer. "But how's he going to get from the middle of Brazil—in the jungle—to *Buenos Aires?*"

"Good question," Buzzer answered. "But there's one thing we can count on. For sure, *Carlos* will get to Argentina, just as he said he would. Bank on it."

Cincinnati stood, wiped the milk from his chin with a napkin, and announced, "If we want to get there ahead of him, we'd better get going. Especially if we want to have a little time to rest."

"We'll need that," Buzzer said.

With that, the little group headed back to *The Flying Pig Machine* and the second half of their ten-hour flight to meet *La Capitán Pérez* and *Teniente* Chuck in Buenos Aires.

*Do you think Cincinnati got enough fuel at* Guayaquil *to fly all the way to* Buenos Aires? *What about* Carlos? *What else will he blow up before he gets to the Atlantic Ocean? Will he try to rob* Capitán Ramos? *Maybe kill him and sink his boat, too? Will Buzzer and his team get to* Buenos Aires *before the big puma? How will* Carlos *get from the mouth of the Amazon River to* Argentina?

# Aprendamos a Hablar en Español
## by Dusty Louise

*Ustedes ya entienden mucho acerca del tiempo. Ahora, aprendamos más acerca de los alimentos.*[20]

## LOS ALIMENTOS

| In English | *In Spanish* | Say It Like This |
|---|---|---|
| Bread | Pan | PAHN |
| Butter | Mantequilla | mahn-the-KEE-zhah |
| Milk | Leche | LAY-chee |
| Toast | Tostado | tohs-TAH-doh |
| Bacon | Tocino, tocineta | toh-SEE-noh, toh-see-NEH-tah |
| Ham | Jamón | hah-MOHN |
| Waffle | Wafle | WAH-fleh |
| Cream | Crema | CRAY-mah |
| Cheese | Queso | KAY-soh |
| Beef | Bíf | BEEF |
| Fish | Pez | PAYSZ |
| Chicken | Pollo | POH-zhoh |
| Soup | Sopa | SOH-pah |
| Salad | Ensalada | een-sah-LAH-dah |
| Potato | Patata | pah-TAH-tah |
| Rice | Arroz | ah-ROZH |
| Vegetables | Verduras | vair-DOO-rahs |
| Fruits | Frutas | FROO-tahs |
| Water | Agua | AH-wah |
| Salt | Sal | SAHL |

---

20. You know a lot about the weather. Now we'll learn more about food.

| Pepper | Pimiento | pee-mee-IHN-toh |
| Sugar | Azúcar | ah-SOO-car |
| Eggs | Huevos | HWAY-vohs |
| Candy | Bombón, dulce | bohm-BOHN, DOOL-seh |
| Chocolate | Chocolate | cho-co-LAH-teh |
| Beans | Habichuelas, frijoles | ah-bee-CHWAY-lahs, free-HOH-lehs |
| Tomato | Tomate | toh-MAH-teh |
| Grapes | Uvas | OO-vahs |
| Catnip | Nébeda | NAY-beh-dah |

# * Chapter 7 *
## *Buenos Aires: Una Vista Muy Familiar*[1]

*En El Aire Sobre la Selva Tropical*[2]

Departure from *Simón Bolívar* airport in *Guayaquil* had been routine. Dusty took the little Sabreliner up to 31,000 feet and set a southeasterly course at exactly 150 degrees.

It was 6:00 A.M. Hill Country time. They would be in *Buenos Aires* in another five hours, just before lunchtime in the Hill Country, but early afternoon in Argentina.

Buzzer Louis, sitting on the port side next to a window, turned to *los gatitos gemelos anaranjados*[3] and asked a question. "Did you know it will be winter in *Buenos Aires*?"

"Why is that?" Luigi was curious as ever. *"Ayer era junio en las colinas de Texas. Junio no es invierno, mi hermano grande e importante. ¿Por qué es invierno aquí ahora?"*[4]

---

1. Buenos Aires: A Familiar Sight
2. In the Air Above the Rain Forest
3. orange kitten twins
4. "It was June in the Texas hills yesterday. June isn't winter, my big and important brother. Why is it winter here now?

Luisa stood up and clapped. *"Tu lenguaje es muy bueno, hermanito. ¡Bravo, bravo!"* she shouted.[5]

*"¿Por qué, Buzzer, por qué? ¿Cómo? ¡Dígame, Buzzer. Rápido! No entiendo."*[6] Luigi was almost frantic.

*"Porque estamos al sur del ecuador, Luigi. Las colinas de Texas están al norte del ecuador. En el sur, cuando es invierno, en Texas es verano. ¿Entiende, Luigi?"*[7] Buzzer explained the difference in seasons to Luigi and Luisa.

"Oh," Luigi said. "And the water in the toilet goes around the other direction, too. *¿Verdad?*"

"Is that right, Luigi?" Buzzer answered. "How did you know that?"

"From Bart Simpson on television. He called Australia and asked about it. Australia is south of the equator, too. Right?" Luigi said.

Luisa was bored with the conversation. She didn't really care which way water turned when you flushed a toilet. And Bart Simpson wasn't her ideal expert on anything.

She tried to change the subject . . . to her favorite pastime. "Tell us a story, Buzzer. Tell us about the queen, and when you got knighted at Cluckingham Palace. Do they keep chickens there? That's a good story. Cincinnati wasn't there, so he can't tell it to us. Besides," she cast an eye toward to cockpit door to be sure Cincinnati couldn't hear, "you tell better stories."

"You do!" Luigi chimed in. "You tell the best stories! Tell

---

5. "Your language is very good, my little brother. Well done!"
6. "Why, Buzzer, why? How? Tell me, Buzzer. Quickly! I don't understand."
7. "Because we are south of the equator, Luigi. The Texas Hills are north of the equator. In the south, when it's winter, it's summer in Texas. Do you understand?

us about the queen. Pleeeze," Luigi begged, while Luisa struck her "cute" pose.

"Okay, *gemelos*. Just one story. Then I want you to get some sleep. Promise?" said Buzzer.

"*Te lo prometemos, hermano. Promesas solemnes,*"[8] Luisa said seriously.

Buzzer began. "It was a few years ago. Elizabeth II, Queen of England, invited me to Buckingham Palace—not Cluckingham, Luisa, no chickens—where she would name me a knight of the realm for my international crime-fighting work.

"As the U.S. ambassador to Great Britain and I drove up to the foreign visitors' entrance, it was raining. Pouring buckets. The ambassador's tuxedo got soaked as we dashed from the car. Since I wear my tuxedo all the time, I just shook off the rain. We joined a long reception line. I was introduced to this dignitary and that dignitary. And this dignitary's great aunt Hildy. And great aunt Hildy's third cousin, Clive.

"Suddenly I looked up, and I was standing right in front of the queen."

"What did you do then?" Luisa's eyes were as big as walnuts.

"Breathe, Luisa!" Luigi reminded his little sister.

"Well, I bowed from the waist and said, 'Your Majesty,' just as I had been told to do. And you know what happened then? The queen reached down, picked me up and held me as if I were some kind of muff. Still holding me, she made

---

8. "You have our promise, brother. Our solemn promise."

a dreadful little speech, one that completely blew my cover as a secret agent. Her voice sounded like sandpaper on badly tuned violin strings.

"Then she put me down. She took up a huge and heavy broadsword. She tapped me on the shoulder and proclaimed me a knight of the realm."

Buzzer went on. "Just then something really strange happened. This could go in your 'strange' book, Luigi. A little mouse peeped out from the floor underneath the queen's gown. He looked right at me, he did. Well, before I thought, I stuck out my tongue and gave that mouse a real Brooklyn raspberry. A nice wet one. Of course, the press, and particularly the tabloids, accused me of giving the raspberry to the queen. I thought of international incidents. I really did.

"But the luck of the Giaccomazzas was with me once

again. Neither the queen nor the Duke of Edinburgh nor the Prince of Wales noticed my tongue or the mouse. Their noses were so high in the air I think they must have been looking at the ceiling.

"But the ambassador fainted. He had to be taken 'to hospital,' as the Brits say. Still, in the end, I was—and am—a royal knight of the House of Windsor. "

"What happened to him?" Luigi wanted to know. He and Luisa looked worried.

"What happened to whom?" Buzzer was once again stumped by the twins' questions.

"The mouse. Who else?" Luigi answered.

"I don't know, Luigi," Buzzer smiled. "I've often wanted to find him and apologize. There was no good reason for what I did. I guess it was nervous energy at work."

Luisa looked at her big brother proudly and asked, "So will you always be a knight?"

"*Sí, sí. Un caballero. Eternamente,*"[9] Buzzer said.

"*Ahora, mis pequeños. Recuerden bien sus promesas. Es hora de dormir,*"[10] Buzzer reminded the twins.

To his everlasting surprise and complete delight, the twins curled up next to one another. They closed their eyes and were soon fast asleep, keeping their promise of trading a nap for a story.

Buzzer thought, "This is too good to be true." And he pulled down the shade next to his seat to block out the sun, which was just peeking over the horizon far below.

Soon he, too, fell fast asleep.

---

9. "Yes, yes. A knight forever."
10. "Now, my little ones. Remember well your promises. It's time to sleep."

✱  ✱  ✱

*En El Río Amazonas. Otra Vez.*[11]

*Capitán Ramos* checked to be sure. The big cat was asleep, for the moment at least. Two hours had passed since the bombing of the boat docks at *Marañón*, and *Ramos* was certain now that his big cat passenger, whoever he was, was a mean motor scooter indeed.

Carefully putting an earpiece into his left ear, he plugged the other end into his portable radio and turned it on. The volume was ever so low. He tuned it to the only station one could hear along this stretch of the big river. Normally, the radio was connected to an amplifier and speakers so he could hear it above the drone of the diesel engine. Not this time, though.

The big cat had strictly forbidden any amplified sound. In fact, the puma had specifically told the captain not to listen to the radio. At all.

*Ramos* wanted to listen long enough to hear the 9:00 A.M. news, just to see if the two explosions might have been reported yet. He knew the authorities in this region were strict, and pretty fast to react. He wondered if there would be time to slip far enough away before too many questions were asked.

He continued to hug the south shore of the Amazon. But it was daylight now, so there'd be no running in the dark to keep the *Meteoro* from being seen. For the next ten hours or so, he would be visible. Very visible.

---

11. On the Amazon River. Again.

A song finished playing in his ear. Then the news came on. Just as he had feared, the river explosions were the lead news story.

But he didn't expect what came next, and it caused him to panic! The reporter said that local authorities had set up a blockade of more than forty craft spread across the river, from one bank to the other. All river traffic was being stopped and searched. The authorities suspected the explosions were the work of that infamous international terrorist, *Carlos* the Puma!

At the mention of the big cat's name, *Ramos* froze. Suddenly he knew for sure who his passenger was. And he also knew the puma wouldn't hesitate to kill him and sink the *Meteoro*. This big cat was truly scary.

But what could he do? As the cat slept below deck, *Ramos* was headed straight into a police blockade. There was little doubt he would be stopped and even less doubt that the police would find the puma below.

*Ramos* would be in big trouble.

If he kept going, he would be stopped and searched. If he stopped and tied up along the bank, *Carlos* the Puma would be furious. No telling what that crazy puma might do then.

There was no good solution. He was trapped. He could leap off the boat and swim ashore. But the police would find his boat and track him down. The big puma would surely follow him to the end of the earth to get even.

*Ramos* had few choices and those he had were all terrible.

While he was thinking about what was going to happen

to him, he didn't notice the two police speedboats coming toward him from the east. They were almost alongside before he saw them.

There was no escape now. *Ramos* was dead meat.

*"Buenos días, capitán,"* a voice called out from one of the boats. *"Por favor, apague su motor. Gracias, señor."*[12]

What else could he do? *Ramos* shut down his engine and the trawler went dead in the water, moving slowly with the current.

One of the boats pulled alongside and *dos policías* jumped aboard the *Meteoro*. *Ramos* knew both of them from his travels up and down the river. That likely would only make things worse for him. Familiarity breeds contempt, right?

The two officers glanced around the deck, and then one of them started down the stairs to the cabin below.

*Ramos* froze.

Then he shouted out, without thinking. *"¡Cuidado, señor!"*[13]

The policeman looked puzzled.

*"¿Por qué, capitán?"*[14] he asked, staring at Ramos.

"The stairs," *Ramos* said, thinking quickly., "they are very slick. *Están mojadas. Por favor, cuidado."*[15]

*Ramos* almost screamed. He was hoping to wake up the puma and at least give him warning about what was happening.

The officer looked at *Ramos*. He motioned to the other

---

12. "Good morning, captain. Please stop your engine. Thank you, sir."
13. "Be careful, sir!"
14. "Why, captain?"
15. "They are wet. Please, be careful."

policeman to follow him. Both pulled pistols from their belts and slipped quietly down the stairs.

*Ramos* held his breath, waiting for shots, explosions, or some other kind of ruckus. But there was nothing but deafening silence.

After what seemed like an eternity, the two officers came out of the stairwell.

"*Gracias, Capitán Ramos*," one of them said, handing Ramos an oversized card. "If anyone else stops you, just show this to them. It will tell them we have searched your boat, and you will be free to pass."

*Ramos* was stunned. How could the big cat just evaporate into thin air? How could he possibly have hidden down there from the *policía*?

He took a deep breath and pulled out the knife he had hidden in his boot. Then he crept down the stairs.

Should he shout?

Or creep?

Either way, Ramos figured he had about a minute left to live.

As he rounded the corner at the bottom of the stairs, the lights were on. The cabin was empty! The big cat wasn't here at all. In fact, everything looked exactly as *Ramos* had left it.

Except, that is, for one thing.

There was a large envelope on the table in the galley. *Ramos* picked it up. Something was inside it, and there was a note scrawled on the back side. It said, "*Gracias, capitán, por el paseo. Mire adentro.*"[16]

---

16. "Thank you, captain, for the ride. Look inside."

The note was signed *Su amigo para toda la vida, Carlos el Puma.*[17]

*Ramos* tore open the envelope. There it was. A stack of *pesos Argentinos*[18] with a rubber band around them.

The rest of *Ramos'* payment for taking *Carlos* the Puma to the Atlantic—even though they hadn't made it all the way.

"*Increíble*," *Ramos* said aloud. *El puma me asusta mucho. Y luego, me paga todo el dinero. Increíble absolutamente.*[19]

*Ramos* almost skipped up the stairs. He started the diesel and moved out into the current, heading for the Atlantic and his bank in *Río de Janeiro*.

*Ramos* thought, If *Carlos* has escaped from prison, then I have just been pardoned from a certain execution. *¡Aleluyá!*[20]

✳ ✳ ✳

*En el Avión del Cerdo Bailarín. Otra Vez*[21]

"*Ezeiza* tower, this is Sabreliner seven-zero-niner-niner-alpha. We're fifty miles northwest, proceeding direct, requesting clearance to land, please."

Dusty was once again calling an airport tower. This time at *Ministro Pistarini* International Airport in *Buenos Aires*, otherwise known as *Aeropuerto Internacional de Ezeiza*. The

---

17. Your friend for life, Carlos the Puma.
18. Argentine dollars
19. "Unbelievable. The puma scares me a lot. Then pays me all the money. Absolutely incredible."
20. "Hallelujah!"
21. In the dancing pig's airplane. Again.

long flight from HCIA to *Guayaquil* to *Buenos Aires* would be over in a few minutes.

"Sabreliner niner-niner-alpha, we have you on approach. Turn ten degrees to your right and descend to 3,000. When you're ten miles out, begin your final. You are clear to land on runway eleven. Wind is from the north-northeast at six knots, gusting to nine. Temperature is seven degrees Celsius."

"*Bienvenidos a Buenos Aires, señorita.*[22] Taxi to Terminal C."

Cincinnati clicked on the intercom. "We're here, folks. Buckle up. We'll be on the ground in fifteen minutes."

He didn't know it, but the dancing pig was talking only to himself and Dusty Louise. Buzzer Louis, Luigi and Luisa were snoring like chainsaws back in the cabin.

The time was 1:15 P.M. in *Buenos Aires*. 11:15 in Texas. It had been a long day.

*How do you think* Carlos *the Puma escaped from the trawler on the Amazon River? Why do you think he was so nice to Captain* Ramos? *Or was he? How will he get from Brazil to Argentina? Or will he? And what about Cincinnati and Dusty? Do you think they're really tired after flying more than ten hours? Will someone meet them at the airport in* Buenos Aires? *Maybe Chuck? Do you think they'll be ready when* Carlos *shows up?*

---

22. "Welcome to Buenos Aires, miss."

# Aprendamos a Hablar en Español
## by Dusty Louise

*¿Tiene usted hambre? Entiende ahora los nombres de muchos alimentos. Ahora, vamos a aprender más de los días, las semanas, los meses, las estaciones y el calendario.*[23]

## MÁS TIPOS DE TIEMPO[24]

| In English | In Spanish | Say It Like This |
|---|---|---|
| Today | Hoy | OY |
| Yesterday | Ayer | Ah-YAIR |
| Day before yesterday | Anteayer | Ahn-tay-ah-YAIR |
| Tomorrow | Mañana | Mahn-YAH-nah |
| Day after tomorrow | Pasado mañana | Pah-SAH-doh Mahn-YAH-nah |
| This week | Esta semana | AY-stah see-MAH-nah |
| Last week | La semana pasada | Lah see-MAH-nah pah-SAH-dah |
| Week before last | Antesemana | Ahn-tay-see-MAH-nah |
| Next week | La próxima semana | Lah PROAK-see-ma see-MAH-nah |
| Week after next | Una semana después de la próxima | OO-nah see-MAH-nah dehs-PWAYS deh lah PROAK-see-mah |
| This month | Este mes | AY-stee mase |
| Last month | El mes pasado | Ehl mase pah-SAH-doh |

---

23. Are you hungry? You now know the names of many foods. Now, we're going to learn more about days, weeks, months, seasons and the calendar.
24. More kinds of time.

## * Buenos Aires: Una Vista Muy Familiar *

| | | |
|---|---|---|
| Next month | *El próximo mes* | Ehl PROAK-see-moh mase |
| Eight A.M. | *A las ocho de la mañana* | Ah lahsz OH-choh day lah mah-NYAH-nah |
| Noon | *Mediodía* | May-dee-oh-DEE-ah |
| Six P.M. | *A las seis de la tarde* | Ah lahs saysz day lah TAHR-deh |
| Midnight | *Medianoche* | May-dee-ah-NOH-cheh |
| Winter | *Invierno* | Een-vee-AIR-noh |
| Spring | *Primavera* | Pree-mah-VAIR-ah |
| Summer | *Verano* | Vair-AH-noh |
| Fall | *Otoño* | Oh-TOHN-yoh |

# Part Three

## Let the Games Begin

"If it weren't for me, this whole venture would be a failure. I helped fly us here. Cincinnati couldn't have done it all by himself, could he? And I'm the only one of this crew that speaks passable Spanish. *Mi español es perfecto. Me llamo* Dusty Louise. *Muy linda. Y a sus órdenes.*[1]

> —Dusty Louise
> Pretty, impatient and
> insecure younger sister

---

1. My Spanish is perfect. I am Dusty Louise. Very pretty. And at your service.

# * Chapter 8 *
# Una Tribu Indígena:
# La Policía Inteligente[1]

*En La Selva Tropical, al Este de Brasil*[2]

Four years in prison had hardened *Carlos* the Puma. With nothing much to do except think and exercise, he'd toned his muscles and developed endurance for the day, like today, when he would need those qualities.

Loping down a narrow trail through the dense under-growth, *Carlos* knew he had miles to cover before reaching one of his former bases. It was a remote landing strip with a generator and a satellite phone—a place where he could call former associates to fly him out to *Buenos Aires*.

He'd make the call, and then rest for a few hours until help got there.

*Carlos* pushed on. He told himself to maintain a steady

1. A Native American Tribe: Smart Police
2. In the Rainforest, Eastern *Brazil*

pace. He knew he could make the landing strip by nightfall at the end of day three since his escape. With a little luck, he would be in *Buenos Aires* tomorrow.

In four days.

Nobody would believe it could be done. *Carlos* had made a career of being underestimated by rivals. He had always announced the impossible, and then he would beat his own announcements.

As he plunged through the jungle, he had time to think, just as he had during the four years he'd spent in that horrific prison. *Carlos* was smart. Very smart. Out-thinking his rivals had kept him alive and out of jail. That is, until the cat and the pig came along.

As he loped along toward the airstrip he reckoned was about twenty-five miles ahead of him, *Carlos'* thoughts turned to *Capitán Ramos*. He had scared the captain on purpose. *Ramos* had probably worried that he, *Carlos*, might sink the *Meteoro*, kill the captain and even steal back the first half of the money.

*Sí, Carlos* snickered to himself, *Ramos* thought he had *tratado mal al capitán.*[3] *Ramos* had probably even thought *Carlos* the Puma was *un motociclista muy malo. Cierto. Sin duda.*[4]

I am many things, *Carlos* thought. But a simple thief of money? *¡Nunca. Jamás!*[5]

In fact, *Carlos* had never stolen a *peso*. The thought had

---

3. treated the captain badly
4. a mean motor scooter. For sure. Without doubt.
5. Never! Never!

never crossed his mind, troubled though his mind might be at times. *Y la idea a traicionar a un ayudante nunca era buena.*[6]

*No. Carlos no era un traidor. ¡Nunca!*[7]

"I'd like to have seen *Ramos* when he found me missing. And then found the envelope with the rest of the money I promised him. *¡Ai, ya, ya! Yo apuesto que él estaba asustado,*"[8] he said aloud.

*Espero que gaste el dinero sabiamente,*[9] *Carlos* thought. *Él es un buen hombre. Fiel a su palabra. Una persona de confianza. Como yo.*[10]

*Carlos* tucked away *Ramos* and his good traits in the databank in the back of his mind. It pays to be good to people who might be able to help me in the future, he told himself. Someday I'll need help again. *Ramos* will remember me, and, because I did right by him, he will help me once more.

The big cat was so lost in thought that he almost failed to hear the warning signs: noises of intruders into his little world of the moment.

At first there were faraway voices. Then, as they got closer and louder, *Carlos* stopped dead in his tracks. The hair on the back of his neck stood at attention, and he slipped under a tangled vine.

Peeking out from his hiding place, *Carlos* saw them. A group of about ten or twelve men. *Casi desnudo.*[11] They were

6. And the idea to double-cross a helper was simply wrong.
7. No. Carlos was no double-crosser. Never!
8. "Oh, my! I'll bet he was scared!"
9. I hope he spends the money wisely.
10. He is a good man. True to his word. A trustworthy person. Like me.
11. Almost naked.

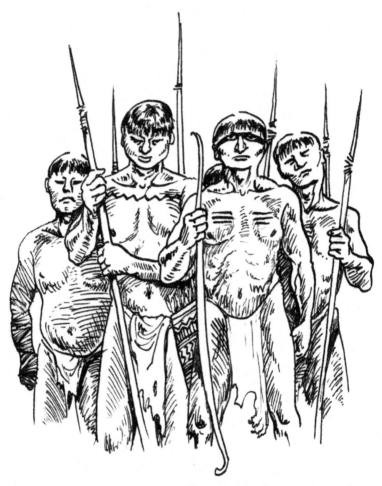

dressed only in loincloths made of animal skins. Muscular and bronzed, they each carried a crude spear, a branch spear with a flint point tied to one end.

One, who seemed to be the leader, carried a primitive bow and wore a handcrafted quiver of arrows. He shouted what seemed to be commands to the others.

*Carlos* thought, *Son indios indígenas. Y cazadores.*[12] Will

---

12. They are indigenous/native Indians. And hunters.

they try to kill me? Or will they be afraid of me? *¿Y, en qué idioma están hablando?*[13]

*Carlos* didn't recognize the language. It wasn't Spanish. It wasn't Portuguese. It wasn't English, or French or German. *Carlos* was fluent in all these languages.

He couldn't make out what the leader was shouting to the others. But the rest of them seemed to respond with the word "*Gris*" each time the leader spoke.

He didn't have time for a face-down with these people. But he could tell they lived very simple lives. *No hay electricidad. Ni teléfonos. Ni computadoras. Agua del río y las lluvias. No hay baños.*[14]

Suddenly he was struck with the thought, They might just be one of those indigenous groups that have never had any contact with the outside world. What a wonderful, simple life they must lead.

As the leader approached where *Carlos* was hiding, the big cat stood and stepped back onto the path. He spoke softly, "*Hola, amigos. ¿Cómo están ustedes? Me llamo Carlos el Puma. No tengo armas. Vengo aquí en paz y tranquilidad.*"[15]

As he spoke, he smiled at the leader. He said, "*Gris. ¿Se llama Gris?*" Then he turned his head and smiled at the rest of the hunters. He counted eight more of them.

They took a couple of steps backward and stared at him as if they had never seen a puma before. It was clear to

13. And, what language are they speaking?
14. No electricity. No telephones. No computers. Water from the river and from rainfalls. No bathrooms.
15. "Hello, my friends. How are you? I am Carlos the Puma. I have no weapons. I come here in peace and tranquility."

*Carlos* they were having trouble understanding what he was saying.

The big cat pointed to his chest. "*Carlos*," he said. He pointed toward the leader, careful not to appear threatening. He asked, "*¿Gris. El jefe?*"[16]

The leader stared back at him. He pointed to the big cat and said, "*Carlos.*" Then he pointed to his own chest and said, "*Gris. El jefe.*"

*Carlos* was pleased. He was making progress talking with them—and they didn't seem to want to shrink his head! Not right away, anyway.

But he didn't have time to chit-chat with these *indios*, no matter how pleasant they might be. He had to get back on the trail to get to the airstrip before dark.

Smiling, he slowly reached into his fanny pack and pulled out a BIC® lighter, the one he used to fire up Molotov cocktails. Holding it upright, he stroked the striker wheel and a flame appeared.

The hunters jumped back, eyes wide. They hummed in unison. Must be some kind of a message to one another, *Carlos* thought.

While the *indios* were still back on their heels, *Carlos* bent down quickly. He scraped together some dried leaves and twigs into a little pile. Then he struck the lighter again and held it to the base of the dry pile. It caught and flared into a tiny campfire.

They stared, amazed, at the fire-stick in *Carlos'* paws

---

16. "Gray. The chief?"

and at the seemingly magic puma who could make fire instantly.

*Carlos* smiled to show he meant the hunters no harm. Then he held the lighter out, offering it as a gift to Gris. "*Un regalo,*"[17] *Carlos* said.

*El Jefe Gris* picked up the lighter. He turned it over and over in his hand. He looked at *Carlos* as if to say, "Where's the fire?"

The puma patiently showed the hunter leader how to turn the striker wheel to make a flame.

*Gris* turned it once. It lit. He dropped the lighter, picked it up, and made another flame. Smiling, he shouted to his party. Then he turned and they all ran pell-mell away from *Carlos*. After about ten steps, though, the hunters stopped in unison. They turned, knelt down on one knee and bowed their foreheads to the ground, as if the big cat were some kind of god.

Or at least a holy magician.

Again in unison they bounded to their feet. They turned and, shouting to one another, they ran down the trail in the direction from which they had come.

*Otro pequeño triunfo, Carlos* said to himself. *Y más amigos para el puma.*[18]

"*¡Adelante!*"[19] he shouted aloud as if talking to his legs.

Then he turned and resumed loping toward the secret landing strip, and his trip on to *Buenos Aires*.

---

17. "A gift."
18. Another little victory. And more friends for the puma.
19. "Forward!"

✱ ✱ ✱

*Al Aeropuerto Internacional Ezeiza en Buenos Aires*

Once on the ground and off the runway, Dusty Louise started to take the controls of *The Flying Pig Machine* to taxi to Terminal C as the air traffic controller had asked her to do.

Cincinnati said gently, "There's way too much ground traffic here, Dusty. Maybe I'd better take us to the terminal park. Not that you couldn't do a great job, but you don't have any experience with ground congestion."

The dancing pig smiled at her.

Dusty was not happy, wondering, How am I supposed to get experience if I don't get to try? An age-old question for beginners of any activity.

Cincinnati parked the little jet on the tarmac next to Terminal C. Two uniformed attendants walked under *The Flying Pig Machine* and set a pair of chocks under the wheels. As if by magic, a Chevron avgas truck appeared to fill up the tanks, even before anybody asked.

Dusty Louise was impressed. "Are they always this helpful?" she asked Cincinnati.

"At most airports in most countries, yes," he said. "The Hispanics are particularly helpful to foreign visitors. They seem to want us to feel welcome as we visit their home."

Back in the cabin, Buzzer Louis' satellite phone chirped.

Buzzer was still asleep, so Luigi, ever the prankster, answered.

"*Hola. Y Listo. ¿Quién es? Por favor.*"[20]

"This is Chuck, just-plain-Buzzer," came a voice. "I am

---

20. "Hello. And ready. Who is this, please?"

in the Terminal C, and I can see your plane. The Sabreliner seven-zero-nine-nine-alpha. *¿Verdad?*"[21]

Luigi wasn't sure whom he was talking to. Nobody had told him and Luisa about Chuck and *la Capitán Paloma.*

"*¿Mira Carlos el Puma? Está allá contigo?*"[22] Luigi asked, winking at Luisa. She was grinning at him, wondering just what he might say next.

"No, just-plain-Buzzer. He couldn't be here yet," Chuck said, and added, "I've come to pick you up and take you all to *la Capitán Pérez*'s office. Your voice sounds much different today, just-plain-Buzzer. Are you okay?"

Luigi couldn't keep from laughing.

He looked at Luisa and then at the cockpit door to be sure Cincinnati and Dusty weren't about to walk back into the cabin and catch him in one of his pranks. Luisa spun her right front paw in the air as if to say, "Go for it, little brother."

So he did.

"*No soy solamente* Buzzer Louis *a secas. Soy* Luigi Panettone Giaccomazza *a secas. El gatito que causa sensación. Aquí conmigo está mi hermana* Luisa Manicotti Giaccomazza *a secas. Somos gemelos. Gemelos muy ingeniosos,*"[23] Luigi said, trying to keep a straight face. "*También con nosotros está nuestro hermano,* Buzzer Louis *a secas, el héroe internacional. Pero él duerme ahora mismo.*"[24]

---

21. "Right?"
22. "Do you see Carlos the Puma? Is he there with you?"
23. "I am not just-plain-Buzzer Louis. I am just-plain-Luigi Panettone Giaccomazza. The sensational kitten. Here with me is my sister, just-plain-Luisa Manicotti Giaccomazza. We're twins. Very clever twins," Luigi said.
24. "Also with us is our brother, just-plain-Buzzer Louis, international hero. But he's sleeping right now."

"*No estoy dormiendo*, Luigi,"[25] Buzzer said as he reached for the phone. He smiled at Luigi to let him know his little prank was okay. Funny, even.

"*Hola*, Chuck. *Soy* Buzzer Louis. Thanks for meeting us. We'll see you on your side of customs in the terminal."

"*Muy bien*, Buzzer *a secas*," Chuck said. He was confused at the conversation with the strange little kitten—so confused, in fact, that he forgot to speak English.

Cincinnati and Dusty popped out of the cockpit. The dancing pig turned the big lever that opened the door and let down the stairs. "Last one out's a smelly puma," he said.

*Do you think Carlos will be able to get to the landing strip before dark? Will he be able to start the generator and make the satellite phone work so he can call for help? What about Chuck? Don't you think he's wondering about why Buzzer brought Luigi and Luisa along? What good are a pair of kitten pranksters when you're tracking down a really bad guy? Will they all get to the Capitán's office? And what will happen there?*

---

25. "I'm not sleeping," Buzzer said.

# Aprendamos a Hablar en Español
## by Dusty Louise

*Ahora ustedes entienden más acerca de sus calendarios. Pero, cuando hace calor en norteamérica, hace frío en suramérica. Entonces, ¿cómo sabemos qué tipo de ropa llevar?*[26]

## TIPOS DE ROPA[27]

| In English | In Spanish | Say It Like This |
|---|---|---|
| Coat | *chaqueta* | Chah-KAY-tah |
| Jacket | *chaqueta* | Chah-KAY-tah |
| Sweater | *suéter* | SWEH-tehr |
| Shirt | *camisa* | Cah-MEE-sah |
| Blouse | *blusa* | BLOO-sah |
| Pants | *pantalones* | Pahn-tah-LOH-nehs |
| Skirt | *falda* | FAHL-dah |
| Dress | *vestido* | Vehs-TEE-doh |
| Suit | *traje* | TRAH-heh |
| Necktie | *corbata* | Cohr-BAH-tah |
| Undershirt | *camiseta* | Cah-mee-SET-tah |
| Underwear | *ropa interior* | ROH-pah een-tear-ee-OHR |
| Raincoat | *impemeable* | Eem-pear-mee-AH-bleh |
| Umbrella | *paraguas* | Pahr-AH-wahs |
| Shoes | *zapatos* | Szah-PAH-tohs |
| Socks | *calcetines* | Cahl-seh-TEE-nehs |
| Boots | *botas* | BOH-tahs |
| Belts | *cinturón* | Seen-too-ROHN |
| Gloves | *guantes* | GWAHN-tehs |

---

26. Now you understand more about your calendars. But when it is hot in North America, it is cold in South America. Then how do we know what kind of clothing to wear?
27. Kinds of Clothing

| Hat | sombrero | Sohm-BREHR-oh |
| Cap | gorra | GOHR-rah |
| Handkerchief | pañuelo | Pahn-WAY-loh |
| Scarf | bufanda | Boo-FAHN-dah |
| Wallet | billetera | Bee-zhea-TEHR-ah |
| Purse | bolsa | BOHL-sah |

# * Chapter 9 *

# Una Sesión Rápida de Estrategia. Y Carlos Llegó Temprano.[1]

*En La Selva Tropical, También*

*Carlos* the Puma knew he was getting close. He could sniff the faint odor of gasoline and fresh paint. *Uno de mis amigos*[2] must have painted the shack where we keep the supplies, he thought as he rounded a corner. And there it all was.

The shack was now a dark green, which made it harder to see from the air, *Carlos* assumed. There was a wide clearing—at least forty meters across—where helicopters could land amid the thick forest. He thought, *La nueva pintura verde es buena idea.*[3]

Night was coming on fast. *Carlos* hurried to place flares around the outside of the clearing. He would light them when he heard the helicopter coming to get him. *"El he-*

---

1. A Quick Strategy Session. And Carlos was early.
2. One of my friends
3. The new green paint is a good idea.

*licóptero vendrá en la noche,*"[4] *Carlos* said aloud, even though there was no one to hear him. *Nada pero insectos y algunos monos en los árboles.*[5]

He lit a kerosene lantern with some matches he found in a small metal box. Then he poured gasoline from a can into the tank of a portable generator. He checked to be sure the little engine was full of oil, closed the choke and pulled the starter four times until it fired and began to run.

Then he plugged in the charger on the satellite telephone in a cabinet, right where it was supposed to be. He would charge it up enough *para telefonar a sus amigos para venir a la selva en un helicóptero. Y transportarlo a Buenos Aires.*[6]

His chores done for the moment, *Carlos* sat down to eat some dried food he'd stored in the shack for days like today as he waited for the satellite phone to charge up. He needed to make the call that would get him to *Buenos Aires* so he could get even with the cat and pig who'd trapped him four years ago and sent him to the terrible prison up the Amazon.

\* \* \*

*Al Aeropuerto Ezeiza*

As *los cuatro gatos tejanos y su amigo, el cerdo bailarín,*[7] climbed down from *The Flying Pig Machine*, they were met by a customs agent, who welcomed them to Argentina. She

---

4. "The helicopter will come at night."
5. Nothing except insects and some monkeys in the trees.
6. to telephone his friends to come to the forest in a helicopter, and take him to Buenos Aires.
7. The four Texan cats and their friend, the dancing pig

said she would escort them through passport control and customs, adding, "*Un policía de nombre 'Chuck' está en el edificio. Él espera allí por ustedes. ¿Sí?*"[8]

Before anybody else could answer, Luigi—hoisting his *mochila amarilla*[9] over his shoulder—asked the agent, "Would that be 'Just-Plain-Chuck' of the Argentinean Federal Police, señora?"

Dusty glared at him. Luisa snickered and Buzzer Louis just smiled. "That was classic, Luigi, just being Luigi, *es todo,*"[10] Buzzer thought.

The customs agent led *el grupo de los cuatro gatos tejanos y el cerdo bailarín*[11] across the tarmac toward a door that was painted blue. The wind had whipped up, and it was chilly outside *The Flying Pig Machine.* Luigi and Luisa clung tightly to their *mochilas* and bent forward against the force of the wind.

Still, the sky was bright blue, and there were only a few puffy little clouds floating lazily overhead.

The agent took out a set of keys and opened a door marked with a sign reading *Para Oficiales Solamente.*[12] She led them up a narrow staircase to a waiting room lit by overhead fluorescent lights.

"I hate standing in line," the ever-impatient Dusty Louise offered. She had noticed there were three lines, each several travelers long. One was marked *Pasaportes*

---

8. "A policeman named 'Chuck' is inside the building. He waits for you there. Right?"
9. yellow backpack
10. that's all
11. the group of four Texan cats and the dancing pig
12. For Officials Only.

*Argentinos.*[13] A second was marked *Otros Pasaportes.*[14] And the third was marked *Personal de Tripulación Solamente.*[15]

The agent looked down at her. "*No es necessario para nosotros esperar en la cola,*"[16] she reassured the gray tabby. Then she smiled and led them around the lines through a second door and into a small office. There, another agent looked at their passports and stamped them. He asked Buzzer Louis, "*¿Por qué vienen a Argentina y Buenos Aires, Señor Gato Blanco y Negro?*"[17]

Buzzer smiled and answered simply, "*Para ayudar a su policía, señor.*"[18]

"*Ah, sí,*" the agent said, relaxing and smiling as if he'd been expecting them—and as if he had just recognized them as the *equipo norteamericano*[19] that Chuck was waiting for. He reached across his small desk and pushed a button on what looked like an intercom. Speaking into it, he said, "*Señor* Chuck, *sus ayudantes desde Texas están aquí. Viene a mi oficina, por favor.*"[20]

The office door swung open almost at once. A tall young man with black hair, a tidy mustache, and bright blue eyes stepped in, wearing a pinstriped suit. "Hello, my friends. I'm Chuck. *Capitán Paloma* and I are really happy to see you." Chuck turned to the agent behind the desk, smiled

---

13. Argentinean Passports
14. Other Passports
15. Flight Crews Only
16. "It's not necessary for us to wait in line."
17. "Why do you all come to Argentina and Buenos Aires, Mr. Black and White Cat?"
18. "To help your police, sir."
19. North American team
20. "Mr. Chuck, your helpers from Texas are here. Come to my office, please.

and said, *"Muchas gracias, Enrique. Nosotros tenemos mucho trabajo hoy y en los días que vienen. Ahora vamos a la oficina de La Capitán Paloma para una sesión rápida de estrategia."*[21]

Chuck turned to his visitors. "Come with me, please. I hope your flight was pleasant." He reached down and patted Luigi and Luisa lightly on their heads—a sort of "welcome to Argentina" action. Endearing.

Luigi looked up at him. "Careful, just-plain-Chuck. Luisa and I may look like cute little kittens to you. And you're right, of course. We are cute little kittens. *Pero somos detectives muy astutos también."*[22]

Luisa cocked her head and batted her eyelashes, giving Chuck her best "cute" look and adding with a wicked smile, *"No subestime a los gatitos gemelos anaranjados,* Chuck *a secas."*[23]

Luigi laughed out loud. Buzzer and Cincinnati smiled. Dusty frowned and tried to pretend she'd never seen the two little scamps before. Ever.

---

21. "Many thanks, Henry. We have a lot of work to do today and in the days to come. Now we're going to Captain *Paloma*'s office for a quick strategy session."
22. But we're also very capable detectives.
23. "Don't underestimate the orange tabby kitten twins, just-plain-Chuck."

Chuck, looking somewhat surprised, turned and led the way to his car, which was parked nearby.

Cincinnati had the thought, Our work here's about to begin.

✳ ✳ ✳

*En La Selva Tropical Otra Vez*[24]

*Carlos* heard the pop-pop-popping of helicopter rotors in the distance. He hurried out of the green shack. He raced around the helicopter clearing beside the long dirt landing strip, setting off flares one after another, until there was a bright circle glowing on the ground. The crew in the helicopter would have no problem making a safe landing.

As the sound of the rotors' blades cutting the thick rain forest air grew louder, *Carlos* also heard the high-pitched whine of the aircraft's two jet engines. As he looked up through the clearing, he saw the French Aérospatiale Dauphin, his own personal airship. Posing as an Argentinean military buyer, he had bought it brand new in France five years before.

The A-Dauphin was a sturdy craft. *Carlos* knew that for sure. That's why he bought it. Designed for the French navy as a search and rescue vehicle, it would do its rescuing tonight. Its searching, in this case, was all over as it dropped softly into the middle of the ring of flares.

*Carlos*, of course, had bought the military version of the Dauphin. Then he had the inside stripped out and replaced with luxurious leather seats, a small galley for in-flight re-

---

24. In the rain forest again

freshments, and all the latest technology. It carried no armaments; that wasn't *Carlos'* style. No rockets. No missiles. No machine guns. Not even an automatic pistol. *Carlos* the Puma preferred to work with more simple weapons: Molotov cocktails, dynamite, and flame throwers.

Ever cautious, *Carlos* watched from behind a stand of huge trees as the rotors wound down and came to rest. The doors opened and his pilot and co-pilot stepped out onto the grassy surface of the landing site. It was dark, but *Carlos* finally saw two men he recognized and admired. Two *amigos* whom he knew he could trust with his life.

With a stealth that was uncanny, unnatural even, *Carlos* stepped into the light of one of the flares and greeted the men who would carry him away from the insects and monkeys and back to civilization where he would get even with that tuxedo cat and his dancing pig sidekick.

Quickly and without speaking a word, *Carlos* and his two helpers turned off the gasoline generator. They locked up the satellite phone. Then they snuffed out all but one of the flares, leaving just enough light to allow them to lock the green shed and, shortly, to climb aboard the luxurious helicopter. Then they filled the airship's fuel tank with a long hose from barrels of jet fuel stashed behind the shed.

It was just after eleven o'clock at night. The landing site was about 850 miles north of *Brasilia*, the capital of Brazil. Starting with a full tank of jet fuel, the Dauphin could reach *Brasilia* in just under five hours, allowing for one fuel stop. *Carlos* thought they could be in the city before sunup.

There I will disguise myself, he thought. Maybe I will become *un vendedor de caballitos para los niños. Y entonces volaré a Buenos Aires como este vendedor. Sí. Es una buena idea. Carlos, tú eres muy ingenioso.*[25]

"*¿Listo Carlos, mi amigo?*"[26] the pilot asked as they climbed into the plush Dauphin.

"*Sí, amigo. ¡Vámonos! Volamos a Brasilia. Dormiré por tres o cuatro horas,*"[27] *Carlos* answered. Then he leaned back and turned one of the plush leather seats into a recliner. He set about getting some much-needed rest as the helicopter lifted into the black night sky, climbing to 1,500 feet and turning to a heading of 176 degrees.

Five hours to *Brasilia, Carlos* thought just before dropping into a deep slumber.

✳ ✳ ✳

*En El Móvil de Policía Con Chuck En Buenos Aires*

Luigi and Luisa were excited, but they were not happy. Seems Chuck's Fiat police cruiser's windows were too high for them to see out on the drive from the *Ezeiza* airport to *La Capitán Paloma*'s office. The two *gatitos* had to buckle up *los cinturones.*[28]

They could only see upward out the side windows, catching a glimpse of an occasional tall building. Nothing else.

"Rats, Luisa," Luigi complained softly. "We fly all night—8,000 kilometers. And for what? To look slantways

---

25. a children's rocking horse salesman. And then I will fly to Buenos Aires as that salesman. Yes, it's a good idea. Carlos, you are very clever.
26. "Ready Carlos, my friend?"
27. "Yes, friend. Let's go! We'll fly to *Brasilia*. I'll sleep for three or four hours"
28. seat belts

at the sky? I haven't even gotten to flush a toilet yet. I want to be sure the water turns clockwise. Or is it the other way?"

"Are we there yet?" Luisa piped up, ignoring Luigi and asking the question every small fry asks from the back seat of the car.

"It will take another few minutes, Luisa *a secas*,"[29] Chuck answered from the driver's seat. "This traffic is heavy, *gatita*, but we don't have much farther to go."

Just then Chuck's cell phone chirped.

"*Hola. Listo. Aquí el Teniente Chuck,*"[30] he spoke into the little clamshell *teléfono*.[31] He listened intently, occasionally uttering an "uh-huh" or a "*sí.*" Finally he said, "*Adios.*"[32]

Closing up the phone and clipping it back to his belt, he turned to Buzzer Louis. "Buzzer *a secas*, that was *La Capitán Pérez*. She wishes our work to be—how do you say?—'confidential?' *¿Verdad?*"[33]

Dusty Louise, claiming her role as interpreter, answered, "'Confidential' is correct, or maybe 'secret.'"

"Yes, *sí.* 'Secret.' That's it. She asks that instead of meeting at her office where there are many eyes and ears, we should meet at your hotel. We have reserved a nice suite of rooms for you at the Sheraton downtown," Chuck said.

"Are we there yet?" Luisa asked again, causing Luigi to snicker and Dusty Louise's eyes to roll.

"Almost, Luisa," Chuck said from the front seat. "We are

---

29. just-plain-Luisa
30. Hello. Ready. Lieutenant Chuck here.
31. Telephone
32. "Goodbye."
33. "True?" or "Right?"

much closer to the Sheraton than to our offices, as a matter of fact. How about six minutes—*seis minutos?* Will that be soon enough for you?

"Then you'll be able to see the sights of our beautiful city," Chuck said. "Did you know *Buenos Aires* is often called 'the Paris of *américa del sur?*'"[34] He was trying to keep the twins occupied until they arrived at the hotel.

Cincinnati said to himself, That Chuck is pretty good with the twins. I wonder if he has any children of his own.

As the dark blue unmarked police Fiat pulled into the drive in front of the Sheraton Hotel, Buzzer Louis glanced out the window. He saw the big fountain, plumes of water shooting high into the air. Then he froze. He started shaking, eyes closed, and put his front paws over his eyes.

Cincinnati noticed his friend's reaction to the fountain where he had almost drowned four years before. He swore to himself he would, once and for all, help Buzzer get over the trauma of the fountain, and get over that night of the tango and wine-tasting contest.

*Will Buzzer Louis ever be able to forget almost drowning in the Sheraton's fountain? Will Cincinnati really be able to help him? And what of Luisa and Luigi? Will they now get to see the sights of Buenos Aires? And why do you think La Capitán Paloma Pérez wants their strategy session and their work to be secret?*

---

34. South America

# Aprendamos a Hablar en Español
## by Dusty Louise

Los cuatro gatos tejanos y el cerdo bailarín viajan por todo el mundo. Es importante saber todos los tipos de transportación. Aquí están algunas palabras acerca de viajes.[35]

| In English | In Spanish | Say It Like This |
| --- | --- | --- |
| Airplane | Avión | Ah-vee-OHN |
| Train | Tren | TREHN |
| Car | Auto | Ah-OO-toh |
| Police car | Móvil | MOH-veel |
| Ship | Barco | BAHR-coh |
| Bus | Autobús | Ah-OO-toh-BOOS |
| Boat | Bote | BOH-tay |
| Truck | Camión | Cah-mee-OHN |
| Pickup | Camionetta | Cah-mee-oh-NET-ah |
| Bicycle | Bicicleta | Bee-see-CLAY-tah |
| Helicopter | Helicóptero | Ay-lee-COHP-tare-oh |
| Road/highway | Camino | Cah-MEE-noh |
| River | Río | REE-oh |
| Street | Calle | CAH-zhay |
| Sea | Mar | MAHR |
| Stream | Arroyo | Ah-ROY-yoh |
| Sidewalk | Acera | Ah-SAIR-ah |
| Path | Senda | SEHN-dah |
| airport | Aeropuerto | Ah-air-oh-PWAIR-toh |

---

35. The four Texan cats and the dancing pig travel all over the world. It's important to know all types of transportation. Here are some words about travel.

# * Chapter 10 *
# Un Proyecto Diabólico Por El Vendedor de Caballitos[1]

*Al Hotel Sheraton en el Centro de Buenos Aires*[2]

"I can't stay in this hotel." Buzzer turned to Chuck as the lieutenant pulled to a stop in front of the Sheraton Hotel next to the dreaded fountain. "Please don't ask me why, Chuck, but isn't there somewhere else we could stay and meet with *La Capitán Paloma?*"

---

1. A Diabolical Plan for the Rocking Horse Salesman
2. At the Sheraton Hotel in downtown *Buenos Aires.*

Chuck looked at Buzzer, then at Cincinnati. The dancing pig shrugged as if to say, "We'll talk later, Chuck."

Chuck turned back to Buzzer. "We could move your reservations to the Hotel Sheraton *Libertador*, just-plain-Buzzer," he said. "It's only a few blocks away. Do you think that would be okay?" Chuck turned again to Cincinnati, who gave him a quick hoof-up. So the lieutenant started the dark blue Fiat cruiser and pulled back into traffic.

"Are we there yet?" Luisa asked for the third time. "You said six minutes, just-plain-Chuck, and it's been more than that. I'm sure it's been at least seven minutes."

Luigi stifled a laugh as Dusty Louise put her front paws over her face and gave a big sigh, expressing extreme impatience with her little sister.

Chuck took out his cell phone and speed-dialed *la Capitán Paloma*'s office to tell her of the change of location.

Buzzer, still distracted, said to Cincinnati, "Would you give a call to Dr. Buford Lewis and his very smart brother Bogart-BOGART back at home to let them know we've gotten here safely? I promised to call once we arrived. Thanks, Cincinnati," he said as he handed the dancing pig his satellite phone.

Chuck, now off his phone, said to Luisa, "See? Here we are." He pulled up in front of a different hotel this time—the Sheraton *Libertador*. "Sit tight while I go in and change the reservations . . . and be sure this hotel has a nice suite for you to stay in while you're all helping us."

As Chuck left the car and walked to the hotel's front door, Cincinnati's call to the little ranch in the Texas Hill Country connected. The dancing pig pushed a small button so everyone left in the police cruiser could listen on speaker phone.

"*Hola. ¿Quién es, por favor? Yo soy el Señor* Bogart-BOGART, *un perro muy inteligente,*"[3] came the greeting from Texas.

"It's Cincinnati and the whole gang, Bogart-BOGART. We're just calling to tell you we arrived safely in *Buenos Aires* a few minutes ago. We'll be staying at the Sheraton *Libertador* Hotel *en la Avenida Cordoba en el centro de Buenos Aires.*"[4]

Cincinnati paused, a puzzled look on his face. Then he said to Bogart-BOGART, "*Habla usted Español conmigo?*"[5]

Bogart-BOGART laughed. "*Hablo un poco solamente, amigo.*[6] I've been practicing that line all morning because I knew you would call soon. Dr. Buford and I have seen the news about the bombings in Brazil. We're sure *Carlos* is behind them and on his way. At least you guys beat him to *Buenos Aires*, Cincinnati," the very smart dog said. "How was the flight?" he added.

"Routine," Cincinnati answered. "We'll call from time to time to keep you and Dr. Buford posted on our progress. Everyone here says 'hello' to both of you. And, Bogart-BOGART," he added. "Keep practicing your Spanish. You never know when it might come in handy. So long, now." Cincinnati clicked the phone shut.

*Teniente* Chuck and a bellman in a charcoal gray suit

---

3. "Hello. Who is this, please? I'm Bogart-BOGART, a very smart dog."
4. on Cordoba Street in downtown Buenos Aires.
5. "Do you speak Spanish with me?"
6. "I speak only a little, friend."

approached the car. Chuck pushed a button on his key ring, and the car's trunk popped open so the bellman could pick up *las mochilas y valijas de los viajeros de Norteamérica.*[7]

Chuck leaned into the front passenger window next to Buzzer Louis and said, "No problem, *mis amigos.*[8] You're all checked in to a nice suite on the twenty-first floor. Just show your passports at the reception desk, and we can go straight to the room. The hotel manager has sent up *un cesto de frutas y algunas meriendas*[9] for you.

"*La Capitán Pérez* will be with us shortly."

Chuck and the bellman led the way from the reception desk where the four Texas cats and the dancing pig showed their passports. They all took an elevator to the twenty-first floor, and the bellman led them into a beautiful suite.

The fruit basket and snacks had already arrived and been set up on a glass table near the windows. Luigi looked at Luisa. She returned his stare, giving him her best 'I dare you' expression. Without a word, they both sprinted to the glass table for a nibble. It had been a long time since breakfast in *Ecuador,* and the *pequeños gemelos anaranjados*[10] were hungry.

"Don't be pigs!" Dusty shouted at them, forgetting about Cincinnati, who gave her a frown and a wink to show he wasn't offended by her unfortunate reference to himself and his fellow porkers.

As the bellman left, he passed a tall, thin woman who

---

7. the North American travelers' backpacks and suitcases
8. my friends
9. a fruit basket and some afternoon snacks
10. little orange twins

turned into the doorway and walked into the room. Dressed in a light gray business suit, she had straight black hair pulled back tightly, and eyes as black as night.

"*Buenos tardes, amigos*,"[11] she said with a friendly smile that only partially hid the worry lines around her eyes and mouth. She clearly had something serious on her mind.

"*Soy La Capitán Paloma Pérez*,"[12] she said. "*Bienvenidos a Argentina y a nuestra ciudad.*"[13]

*Teniente* Chuck introduced Buzzer, Dusty, Cincinnati and the twins. *La Capitán Paloma* cast a glance at Luigi and Luisa that said, "Why are these babies along on this mission? We have serious problems to solve here."

The twins didn't miss the look she gave them. Luigi, always quick to rise to a challenge, stood up and looked straight at the woman. He put down the cookie he was munching, and said, "*No te preocupes de los gemelos. Luisa y yo somos detectives muy astutos, Capitán. Somos pequeños, pero listos—ayudantes de calidad.*"[14]

Luisa, meanwhile, flashed a defiant look at the *Capitán*.

"*Es verdad, Capitán*,"[15] Chuck said, stepping in to take the edge off Luigi's comments and Luisa's defiance. "These kittens are young and small, but they're veteran criminal catchers. I must tell you some time about how they helped catch that rogue owl, Fred-X."

---

11. "Good afternoon, friends,"
12. "I am Captain Paloma Perez."
13. "Welcome to Argentina and our city."
14. "Don't worry about the twins. Luisa and I are very clever detectives. We are small, but smart—quality helpers."
15. "It's true, Captain."

* *Un Proyecto Diabólico Por El Vendedor de Caballitos* *

*La Capitán Paloma* smiled at Luigi, then at Luisa. *"¡Bravo, gatitos! Entonces, vamos a trabajar"*[16]

Luigi and Luisa beamed at being so quickly accepted and included. But they still had snacks to work on, too. They were sure to sit right next to the glass table, so as not to let work interfere with their snacking.

The twins continued to nibble on the snacks as *la Capitán Paloma* called a strategy meeting to order. Buzzer, Cincinnati, and the *teniente* sat in comfortable chairs in a semicircle facing the *capitán* and the glass table where Luigi and Luisa were busy eating some goodies.

*Teniente* Chuck suggested, "Why don't we start by having just-plain-Buzzer and Cincinnati tell us everything they know about *Carlos*? Then we will have time to put together a plan to capture him. Or perhaps you need to rest, and we'll plan tomorrow. Surely it will take him another day or two to get to *Buenos Aires*. He was only in *Marañon* early this morning. There's no way he can get here for a couple of days, *¿Verdad?*"

Buzzer looked up and smiled. "Let us begin, Chuck, by telling you all we know about *Carlos* the Puma. The first thing you have to understand is never to underestimate him. Yes, he was in *Marañon* early this morning. But we were in *Guayaquil* early this morning, too. And we're not magic, Chuck. But we're here, just seven hours later."

**\* \* \***

---
16. "Good, little cats. Then let's get to work."

*Al Aeropuerto Ezeiza–Mañana Por La Mañana*[17]

In disguise, *Carlos* the Puma was at his very best. He slipped quietly into the immigration line marked *Pasaportes Argentinos.*[18] He carried a large sample case. Inside was a model rocking horse, *un caballito para los niños. Carlos era un vendedor de caballitos hoy.*[19]

And he was in *Buenos Aires*, only a half day behind Buzzer and the gang.

*Carlos*, his passport stamped, walked out slowly, looking up and down the street outside the baggage claim area. There it was. A long black Mercedes limousine, his own private car. *Carlos* opened the back door and tossed in his sample case. Then he climbed into the back seat and said to his chauffeur, "Let's go to the Sheraton *Libertador* downtown. That'll be a good base from which to track down that cat and his pig friend."

The driver asked, "What makes you think they will be in *Buenos Aires*?"

---

17. At Ezeiza Airport—The Next Morning
18. Argentinean Passports
19. A rocking horse for the children. Carlos was a rocking horse salesman today.

*Carlos* replied, "Oh, they will be here all right. You can bet on it. Those two are dedicated to keeping me locked up, for sure. But I, *Carlos* the Puma, I will have *una sorpresa grande*[20] for them. You can bet on that, too, *amigo*."

* * *

*En El Vestíbulo del Hotel Sheraton Libertador.*[21]

*Carlos* approached the registration desk in the hotel lobby. A bellman beside him carried his sample case with the model rocking horse inside.

"*Por favor*," he said politely to the desk clerk, "I will have my usual suite, *Guillermo*."

The clerk knew *Carlos* only as a traveling salesman who sold many different products from time to time—Chinese shoes, rocking horses, glassware from Venice, jewelry from Switzerland.

*Guillermo* put on a worried face. "*Lo seinto, Señor Vendedor. Cuatro gatos y un cerdo bailarín de Norteamérica están en su suite de acostumbre. Usted no tiene reservación hoy. Lo siento mucho.*"[22]

The clerk looked almost scared, as if he knew he was about to suffer major abuse at the hands of a very disappointed regular customer.

But *Carlos* only smiled. In fact, he looked pleased. Smug, even. "*No hay problema, amigo mío*,"[23] *Carlos* said. "*Es perfecto.*

---

20. a big surprise
21. In the Lobby of the Sheraton *Libertador* Hotel
22. "I'm sorry, mister salesman. Four cats and a dancing pig from North America are in your usual suite. You have no reservations today. I'm very sorry."
23. "It's not a problem, my friend."

*Dame otro cuarto. Así son las cosas,*"[24] he smiled at a very relieved *Guillermo*, who scrambled to find the next best suite in the hotel for his regular customer, *el vendedor. El vendedor de los caballitos para los niños hoy.*[25]

As he followed the bellman to the elevator, *Carlos* thought, Can it really be this easy? He laughed out loud. A wicked laugh that startled the bellman.

*Do you think Luigi and Luisa will eat too many snacks? What about* Capitán Paloma? *Does she believe the tiny orange twins are really good detectives? Will Cincinnati or Dusty figure out that* Carlos *is staying in the same hotel as they are? Or maybe it will be Buzzer or the twins. And what of* Carlos? *He knows where the Texas cats and the dancing pig from Ohio are staying, but they don't know where he is. Will he be ready to get even with Buzzer and Cincinnati before they even know he's right there with them?*

---

24. "It's perfect. Give me another room. That's the way it is."
25. the salesman. The children's rocking horse salesman today.

# Aprendamos a Hablar En Español

by Dusty Louise

Entiende muchas palabras acerca de la transportación. Ahora, vamos a aprender más acerca de los hoteles.[26]

| In English | In Spanish | Say It Like This |
| --- | --- | --- |
| Hotel | Hotel | oh-TELL |
| Lobby | Vestíbulo | vess-TEE-boo-loh |
| Clerk | Funcionario | foon-see-oh-NAHR-ee-oh |
| Bellman | Botones | bow-TOH-nehs |
| Elevator | Elevador, Ascensor | ay-lee-vah-DOHR, ah-sehn-SOHR |
| Single Room | Habitación | ah-bee-tah-see-OHN |
| Double Room | Habitación doble | ah-bee-tah-see-OHN DOH-bleh |
| Suite | Suite | SWEE-teh |
| Room Service | Servicio de habitación, or Room Service | Sair-VEE-see-oh day ah-bee-tah-see-OHN (Many Hispanics simply use English words) |
| Bathroom | Cuarto de baño | KWAHR-toh day BAHN-yoh |
| Towels | Toallas | toh-AHL-lahs |
| Sheets | Sábanas | SAH-bah-nahs |
| Pillows | Almohadas | ahl-moh-HAH-dahs |
| Wakeup Call | Servicio de desperador | sair-VEE-see-oh day dehs-pair-ah-DOOR |
| Restaurant | Restaurante | res-tah-RAHN-teh |
| Coffee Shop | Café | cah-FAY |

---

26. You understand many words about transportation. Now we're going to learn more about hotels.

| Gift Shop | *Tienda de regulos* | tee-IHN-dah day ray-GAH-lohs |
| To Check In | *Registrarse en un hotel* | ray-jis-TRAHR-say een oon oh-TELL |
| To Check Out | *Irse de un hotel* | EER-say day oon oh-TELL |

# * Chapter 11 *
# Jugando a Las Escondidas en El Hotel[1]

*Carlos Está Dormiendo en El Hotel*[2]

When the bellman took *Carlos* to his room, the puma climbed into the big double bed and quickly fell asleep. His three-and-a-half-day trip from the prison at the headwaters of *el Río Amazonas*[3] had seemed like a week to him. The plotting and planning, the practice explosions, and all the drama of dealing with *Capitán Ramos* had left him tired. Bone-tired. Without even bothering to eat any breakfast, *Carlos* decided his first step in tracking down *los cuatro gatos Tejanos y su amigo, el cerdo bailarín*[4] would be simply to get some sleep.

After all, both of his *metas*[5] had registered and were stay-

---

1. Playing hide-and-seek in the hotel
2. Carlos is sleeping in the hotel
3. the Amazon River
4. the four Texan cats and their friend, the dancing pig
5. targets, or objectives

ing in the same hotel where he was right now. They were staying in his suite *acostumbrado*,[6] right down the hall from his room. In fact, all five of them were within a few meters of the bed he was sleeping on this morning.

*¡Qué buena suerte!*[7] he said to himself as he drifted into a deep sleep.

✳  ✳  ✳

*Pocos Metros de Aquí*[8]

*Carlos'* usual suite at the *Hotel Libertador* was a beehive of hushed activity early in the morning as the puma was checking in and settling down for an early morning nap.

Luigi and Luisa woke up early, refreshed and ready to go after a good night's sleep. At Luisa's quiet urging, Luigi had called room service, impersonating Buzzer Louis' voice, and ordered chocolate cake and vanilla ice cream for two for breakfast. Licking the final crumbs off his whiskers, he said to Luisa, "*Me gusta mucho el helado de vainilla y torta de chocolate.*"[9]

Luisa nodded, adding, "Mmm," in the universal language for "You're so right, Luigi."

Shoving two small, crumb-covered plates and two bowls, spoons and forks under his bed, Luigi turned to his twin sister and

---

6. usual suite
7. "What good luck!"
8. A few meters away
9. "I really like vanilla ice cream and chocolate cake a lot."

noted, "It's best to hide these before Dusty sees them. You know how she is about *desayunos dulces, ¿verdad?*"[10]

Luisa smiled and whispered to her *hermanito,*[11] "You better get the rest of that chocolate icing off your face, Luigi, or Dusty Louise will clean it off for you. And we'll both be in big trouble."

"Let's pretend we're still asleep, Luisa," Luigi suggested. "That way, Dusty will never figure out we had *un desayuno ilegal.*"[12]

Just as the twins climbed back onto the little rollaway beds the hotel had provided for them, Dusty Louise stepped from her bedroom into the little parlor where they were "sleeping."

Almost immediately, Buzzer and Cincinnati came out of the bedroom they had shared, so now all five of them were in the same room.

"Good morning," Dusty said softly to Buzzer and Cincinnati. "Won't you look at those two little darlings still sleeping away? In spite of all the snacks they ate yesterday afternoon, I'll bet they're very hungry. Sometimes when I see them like this, I just want to squeeze both of them in a big hug." She smiled.

Luigi and Luisa couldn't hold back. They laughed out loud.

Luisa batted her eyes, cocked her head and looked up at her big sister and said, "It's okay with us if you want to give us a hug right now, Dusty."

10. sweets for breakfast, right?
11. little brother
12. an illegal breakfast

Luigi added, "We just this instant woke up. Really, we did. We might have slept a long time, too long, if you hadn't come in and started talking to Buzzer and Cincinnati, Dusty. How can we ever thank you enough?"

Luisa buried her head in her *almohada*[13] and quickly slipped under a *sábana*[14] to keep from laughing hysterically, giving away Luigi's brazen claims as bogus.

"Tell you what," Buzzer said, "let's go down to the third floor *café* for some breakfast. Chuck and *la capitán* will be here to pick us up in less than an hour."

Luisa looked at Luigi. She put a paw over her stomach, crossed her eyes and stuck out her tongue. "I don't feel much like eating," she said, adding in a whisper, "again."

✷ ✷ ✷

*A la Boca del Río Amazonas*[15]

*Capitán Ramos* steered the *Meteoro* south of the islands near the mouth of the Amazon River and turned to starboard along the Atlantic coast toward *Belém*, the easternmost point of his regular run—near where the big river emptied into the South Atlantic Ocean.

He was a full day early because of the rush with the big cat upriver. But he wouldn't have to explain his premature arrival to anyone. Probably nobody would even notice if he just tied up and took the day off tomorrow before heading back upriver.

---

13. pillow
14. sheet
15. At the Mouth of the Amazon River

On the other hand, he was torn about what to do next—after he got his money from the puma in the bank, that is. His conscience was hard at work. Should he just keep quiet about what had happened? Likely nobody would ever connect him to *Carlos'* escape and trip down river. But too many people had seen him and the *Meteoro* just before the cigarette boat and the docks at *Marañón* had exploded. Would the authorities want to question him? Or would they, because he regularly ran up and down the Amazon, just chalk it up to coincidence?

Did he owe *Carlos* the favor of keeping quiet since the big cat had paid him in full, even for a job not totally completed? Or should he tell what he knew so the authorities could have a better chance of capturing the puma before he set off another bomb that injured or killed someone?

*Ramos* would spend the night and most of the next day thinking about what to do. By tomorrow afternoon he would decide either to keep quiet or to spill the whole story. Meantime, he had the money to get to the bank. Whatever he did, the money was his.

There was no question about that in his mind. He had bargained for the money with *Carlos*. He had done almost exactly what the big cat had asked. And *Carlos* had paid him in full.

No, he decided. He would not talk about the money to anyone, nor would he give it up.

It was his.

* * *

*En el Café del Hotel Libertador*[16]

"Eat your Cheerios®, you two ragamuffins," Dusty Louise commmanded the tiny twins. "I don't understand why you're not really hungry. C'mon, now, eat up."

Luigi looked at Luisa and whispered, "Wait until Dusty's looking the other way, Luisa. Then hand me your cereal bowl. Our Cheerios are going into this potted plant beside my chair. What kind of a plant is it, anyway?" He asked, changing the subject, as was his habit.

Luisa smiled, inching her bowl toward him. "I think it's called a cereal-eating plant." She winked. "Yes, that's it. Definitely it's a cereal-eating plant. And it looks very hungry, don't you think?" Just then Chuck and the *capitán* walked into the coffee shop. Buzzer and Cincinnati stood up, and Dusty was momentarily distracted.

Luigi quickly dumped both bowls of cereal into the base of the potted plant. "Eat up!" he said to the plant, to Luisa's delight, mocking Dusty's earlier command to them, and they both grabbed napkins to wipe the milk off their faces.

"All done," Luisa announced with a smile as Dusty turned to see what the two of them were doing.

"*Buen trabajo, gemelos,*"[17] Dusty said with a big smile on seeing their empty bowls. "Now we can all get to work finding and capturing *Carlos.*"

"*Buenos días, amigos,*"[18] *Capitán Paloma* said as she walked up to the table where Buzzer, Cincinnati, Dusty, and the twins were sitting. "I have arranged for a soundproof inter-

---

16. In the Coffee Shop in the *Hotel Libertador*
17. "Good work, twins."
18. "Good morning, friends."

rogation room at our headquarters. We can meet there and be assured nobody is listening in. When you're ready, we can go to our offices. Now that you have told us all you know about *Carlos*, we can spend a little time trying to figure out how to capture him once and for all time, no?"

"Please, finish your breakfasts first," Chuck said, adding, "I see that Luigi and Luisa have eaten all their cereal so they will grow up to be big and strong."

"Puleeze, Chuck," Luigi said, smiling at the lieutenant and dragging out the word in exaggeration. "We're full as ticks right now. Probably won't even want any lunch today. Right, Luisa?"

Luisa laughed. "Probably not, Luigi," she said, striking her signature cute pose.

Lieutenant Chuck said to the group, "My car is right outside. *¡Vámonos!*"[19]

✴ ✴ ✴

*Con Carlos el Puma Otra Vez*[20]

Even as tired as he was, *Carlos* slept badly. Tossing and turning, he dreamed about *Capitán Ramos* and the *Meteoro* back on the Amazon River. The cigarette boat, instead of burning and sinking, rose up from the water and fell on top of *Ramos'* trawler, setting it ablaze. He saw *Ramos*, his clothing on fire, jump screaming into the river. And then he saw crocodiles and piranhas racing toward the captain, who

---

19. "Let's go!"
20. With *Carlos* the Puma Again

simply disappeared below the surface in an ever-widening pool of bubbles, and never came back up.

*Carlos* thrashed around on his bed, legs and sheets flying. He groaned, turned and groaned again. This time his dream was of the police boats on the river and the two policemen who just missed seeing him as he slipped over the side rail of the *Meteoro*, wearing a life jacket to keep himself afloat until he could cat paddle to the south shore about a hundred meters away. In his dream, the police heard him splash in the water, and opened fire with Sten machine pistols, riddling *Carlos'* life jacket with dozens of bullets, bullets that were sure to end the work of *Carlos* the Puma.

Forever.

*Carlos* woke up abruptly. He was, in fact, wet. Wet from perspiration brought on by his thrashing and by the stress of reliving very different versions of real-life events on the river. He went into the bathroom and splashed his face with cold water. *Carlos* said to himself, *Estos sueños son locos.*[21] I am safe and sound here in *Buenos Aires*, and that pesky cat and his pig friend are staying right down the hall in my usual suite. They're sitting ducks, so I can just go back to sleep. I need some rest so I'll be alert.

He lay back down on the bed, pulled the damp sheet over himself, buried his head in a pillow and went back to sleep immediately.

✳ ✳ ✳

---

21. These dreams are crazy.

*En La Oficina de La PFA*[22]

The interrogation room was just as the *capitán* had described it. There were no windows. The walls were filled with washed sand to absorb sound. Its door was solid wood, three inches thick, and the walls were painted that same yucky light green favored by government buildings all over the world.

A round table with six chairs stood right in the middle of the room. In front of each chair were a notepad and freshly sharpened pencil. Water glasses sat beside each notepad, and a pitcher of ice water rested on a small tray smack in the middle of the table.

As the team sat down, *Teniente* Chuck spoke. "Yesterday, you were kind enough to tell us a lot about this character *Carlos* the Puma—many things we did not know. Now it's time to figure out how to trap him. So let's begin by telling you what we have done since you arrived. *Capitán?*"

*La Capitán Paloma* began, "Unlike most of the petty criminals we deal with, *Carlos* works hard to avoid being a creature of habit. He is, as you would say, 'unpredictable' most of the time. Still, we will have posted teams at all the airports, train stations, bus terminals and car rental agencies later today. And we will call personally on the management of every nice hotel in the city to ask them to notify us at once if any guest matching the puma's description should check into their hotel. The two or three of his associates who are known to us will be followed, starting today

---

22. At the Headquarters of *Policía Federal de Argentina*

at noon. What else should we do right away, just-plain-Buzzer?"

Buzzer Louis looked across the table at Cincinnati. The dancing pig shrugged his shoulders as if to say, "You say it, Buzzy."

So Buzzer did. "*Capitán* and *teniente*," he began, smiling, "All that you are about to do is excellent police work. I commend you for putting together such an action plan so quickly. But Cincinnati and I believe it all may be too late. You see, we think *Carlos* is very likely already in *Buenos Aires*."

The *capitán* and *teniente* stared at Buzzer, unbelieving. Chuck spoke first. "How can you think he's already here, Buzzer? It just doesn't seem possible."

Cincinnati spoke softly, so softly that everyone found themselves leaning in toward him to be sure to hear what he was saying.

"Normal police procedures work wonderfully with normal criminals. But *Carlos* is anything but a normal criminal. He steals nothing. He refuses to carry a gun or knife. He even considers himself very honorable. No, my friends, *Carlos* is different.

"Very different. He operates on a spectacular scale. His handgun is a flamethrower. His machine pistol is a Molotov cocktail. He's a big planner, who operates in a big way. When he said he'd be here in five days, you can bet he was actually thinking three and a half. "So our job is also to operate on a grand scale—in addition to the usual police procedures, of course. We can't overlook the routine, but we can't expect it to do the whole job, either."

"So where do we go from here?" Chuck asked.

Luigi answered, "Just-plain-Chuck, we must think like the hardened criminal. We must have a plan to match his evil thinking and, as important, his unusually sharp instincts. Remember, this guy's as smart as anybody in this room. Except Luisa, probably," he said, smiling at his little sister.

Buzzer looked proudly at his baby brother. "Well said, Luigi. You are exactly right." He looked around the table. "So, folks, let's start thinking big, and let's begin with a plan that's so grandiose you'll think it's ridiculous."

*La Capitán Paloma* and *Teniente* Chuck each nodded, took off their suit coats, rolled up their sleeves, and grabbed a pencil and notepad. "Let's do it!" the capitán said.

*Do you think Luigi's right? Or does* Carlos *have such an advantage already by knowing where his enemies are that it's too late for grand plans? Do you think* Carlos *might blow up the entire hotel just to get even with Buzzer and Cincinnati? Or maybe make Buzzer go for a swim in the fountain at the other Sheraton, only to torture him?*

# Aprendamos a Hablar en Español
by Dusty Louise

*¿Cómo se llaman las partes del cuerpo?*[23]

| In English | *In Spanish* | Say It Like This |
|---|---|---|
| Ankles | *Tobillos* | Toh-BEE-zhos |
| Arms | *Brazos* | BRAH-zhos |
| Cheeks | *Cachetes* | cah-CHEH-tehs |
| Chin | *Barbilla* | bahr-BEE-zhah |
| Face | *Cara* | CAH-rah |
| Fingers | *Dedos* | DAY-dohs |
| Hair | *Cabello* | Cah-BAY-zhoh |
| Hands | *Manos* | MAH-nohs |
| Head | *Cabeza* | Cah-BAY-sah |
| Hips | *Caderas* | cah-DARE-ahs |
| Lips | *Labios* | LAH-byohs |
| Mouth | *Boca* | BOH-cah |
| Neck | *Cuello* | KWAY-zhoh |
| Shoulders | *Hombros* | OHM-brohs |
| Toes | *Dedos de pies* | DAY-dohs day pee-AYS |
| Tongue | *Lengua* | LEHN-gwah |
| Wrists | *Muñecas* | moon-YEA-cahs |
| Stomach | *Estómago* | ess-TOH-mah-goh |
| Eyes | *Ojos* | OH-hosz |
| Ears | *Orejas* | oh-RAY-hasz |

---

23. How do you say the parts of the body?

# Part Four

# Cat Tracks in the City

"The only way to track down this cat is with a humongous, stupendous, even grandiose plan. I can do that. It's my job."

—Luigi Panettone Giaccomazza
A Very Savvy Little Kitten

"We can catch *Carlos*. I'm sure of it. After all, don't all pumas just smell funny? Follow your nose. That's what I say."

—Luisa Manicotti Giaccomazza
Luigi's Equally Savvy Twin Sister

# * Chapter 12 *
# Un Plan Secreto del Señor Gatito Luigi[1]

*Carlos se Despertó al Mediodía*[2]

Following his bout with nightmares, *Carlos* slept soundly. Over the years he had learned that short naps, even just an hour or two, refreshed him. In his business as a for-hire terrorist, grabbing a short nap often meant the difference between a perfectly carried-out plan and a slip-up that could cost him his freedom. Or even his life.

Yes, a rested body and clear thinking were important to staying alive and out of trouble. *Carlos* was very careful not to allow himself to get too tired.

So at noon, when he woke up, he thought he was ready to get on with his mission to get even with that *gato revoltoso y su amigo, el cerdo bailarín.*[3]

---

1. A Secret Plan from Little Mister Luigi
2. Carlos Woke Up at Noon
3. troublesome cat and his friend, the dancing pig

But first, having skipped breakfast, *Carlos* was hungry. Hunger, like fatigue, could be dangerous to an international terrorist. He picked up the phone and ordered *un almuerzo pequeño*[4] from room service—a salad, shrimp cocktail, and a dinner roll with a glass of milk.

Waiting for the food, he switched on CNN Worldwide. Sure enough, the Brazilian authorities were still speculating that yesterday's bombings along the Amazon River were the work of *Carlos* the Puma. But they had no proof. *Nada.*[5]

*Carlos* smiled to himself. They'll never be able to pin those little *estallidos*[6] on me, he thought. Besides, they were only popgun-sized compared to my usual work. It will never add up if they really think about it.

When *el botones*[7] brought his lunch, *Carlos* took him aside confidentially. He handed the bellman one hundred Argentine *pesos* and struck a deal. The bellman would un-wittingly become his helper.

"Here is what I want you to do, *Jaime*," *Carlos* said. "I was very disappointed this morning not to be able to have my usual suite. *Guillermo* tells me there are four North American cats and a dancing pig staying in it, *¿verdad?* I need you to help me keep track of them. Let me know when they leave the suite and when they return. *¿Comprendes, Jaime?*"[8] *Carlos* said, adding, "There are more *pesos* for you where these came from. You help me keep tabs on the cats and the pig, and I'll reward you handsomely. Got it?"

---

4. a small lunch
5. Nothing.
6. explosions
7. bellman
8. Do you understand, James?

*Jaime* smiled at the puma, patted him reassuringly on the shoulder and said, "You can count on me, *Señor Vendedor*. I will watch them very carefully and report their every movement. Be sure of it."

*Carlos* smiled at him, opened the door for him to leave and then sat down to enjoy his food. This is just too easy, he said to himself. I wonder if I'm missing something here? I'll have to think about it some more—after I finish my lunch.

* * *

*En La Oficina de la PFA*[9]

Everyone sat at attention. Luigi had been talking non-stop for almost an hour as the others grabbed their pencils and pads and made notes—lots of notes.

Suddenly Luigi stood up, dusted his two front paws together and concluded, "That's it. The plan that Luisa and I worked out last night while everyone else was sleeping. A plan so grandiose, yet so simple, it's sure to match *Carlos'* cleverness, and yet it's not complicated for any of us." He paused and looked around the room. "So what do you think?" Luigi gave a smug smile and a wink to his twin.

"*¡Brillante!*"[10] Chuck said emphatically. "Luigi, I think you are truly *un detective genio.*"[11]

*Capitán Paloma* added, "*Lo siento,*[12] Luigi. I admit that yesterday I doubted you and Luisa would be much help in this effort. Well, I was wrong. Really wrong. When you grow up, I will have jobs right here in *Buenos Aires* for the two of you. *Gatos detectives para la PFA,*[13] working with *Teniente* Chuck. *¡Qué equipo!*"[14]

Buzzer Louis swelled with pride in his baby siblings. They were good thinkers, for sure. Cincinnati beamed, also very pleased at Luigi and Luisa's plan.

Even Dusty couldn't keep from smiling. They were growing up, though Dusty wasn't sure that was such a good thing.

---

9. In the Office of the Argentine Federal Police
10. Brilliant!
11. a detective genius
12. I'm sorry
13. Cat detectives for the Argentinean Federal Police
14. What a team!

Before she worried too much about it, though, Luisa piped up, "Now can we have some *helado de chocolate, por favor?*"[15]

"Maybe they weren't growing up too fast, after all," thought Dusty.

"Yes, we'll all have some ice cream in a few minutes," Buzzer said. "But first, we need to be sure Chuck and *la capitán* have a complete list of all the things we'll need to follow your plan. Luisa, would you please go over them for us?"

Luisa stood in her chair, mostly so she could see over the table, but also to take her rightful place in the spotlight. She and Luigi had drawn straws last night to see who would get to tell everyone about the stupendous plan, and she had lost. Although, to this moment, she was convinced Luigi had somehow cheated.

"Right, Buzzy," she began. "Here's what we'll need:

* A car, an old junker that will be almost invisible on the streets, but one that's in great running shape and will go very fast if we need it to.
* Two Vespas, one each for Luigi and me, of course.
* New skateboards for Cincinnati, Buzzer, Dusty and Chuck.
* Disguises for Buzzer and Cincinnati, since *Carlos* will recognize them. How about *gauchos*?[16]
* A helicopter and two-way radios to keep track of

15. chocolate ice cream, please
16. cowboys

action from overhead. Cincinnati can fly it. Dusty can help."

Luisa smiled. "That's about it, I think. Anything else, Luigi?" she asked.

"Only some smaller things that may come up as we go, Luisa—scissors, tweezers, a stun gun, some chocolate ice cream." Luigi smiled wickedly.

*Capitán Paloma* clapped her hands. "I think these two little geniuses deserve a break and some chocolate ice cream right now. Chuck, will you take them to the *cantina*[17] while I fill out the paperwork to get the car, the motor scooters, skateboards, and the disguises, and also line up a helicopter? The rest of us will join you there in *diez minutos*."[18]

She turned to Cincinnati. "Can you fly a Bell Jet Ranger, Cincinnati? We have four of them here in the city."

"*Sí, capitán. Es muy fácil volar*,"[19] Cincinnati answered. "I have logged many hours flying Jet Rangers. That'll be fine. Thank you." Chuck grabbed Luigi and Luisa by a front paw each. "Let's go get that ice cream, you two. I think I'll have *helado con fresas*."[20]

* * *

*Carlos, El Merodeador*[21]

*Carlos* finished his lunch, brushed his teeth and slipped quietly into the hallway. Locking his own room, he crept

---

17. mess hall, or dining room
18. ten minutes
19. "Yes, captain. It's very easy to fly."
20. ice cream with strawberries
21. *Carlos, the Prowler*

past his usual suite, noting only the number of paces between it and his door: nineteen. That info would come in
handy if he got Jaime to pull the master electrical switch,
blacking out the entire floor.

Now it was time for him to close his eyes and memorize
every detail of the entire floor. He must be able to move,
and move quickly, in total darkness. His plan had not taken
shape yet, but he knew it would involve working in the
dark. It always did. That's the world of for-hire terrorists—
stealth and darkness.

Eyes closed, *Carlos* came to the end of a hallway near the
elevators. He could sense by a slight updraft of air that one
of the elevator doors was open. He moved cautiously, but
deliberately.

Suddenly he bumped into something—or someone.
Retreating two steps and opening his eyes quickly, he saw
*Jaime* standing in front of him wearing a big smile.
"*Perdóneme, Señor Vendedor,*"[22] the bellman said. "I have come
to report on the cats and the dancing pig."

*Carlos* nearly panicked. While he had sensed the open
elevator door, somehow he had completely missed the smell
and warmth of a human being right next to him. Am I losing my touch? he wondered. Have I been in prison so long
that my senses are dulled? This will never do! I have to get
better than this before I take on that pesky cat and the pig.

Forcing himself to remain calm, he asked *al botones*,[23]
"What is your report?"

"The cats and the pig left about 9:00 this morning with

---

22. "Excuse me, Mister Salesman."
23. the bellman

a captain and lieutenant of the PFA. They have not yet returned, but I'll let you know as soon as they do."

"Thank you, *Jaime*." *Carlos* resumed his prowl, and this time he was more alert.

As the bellman returned to the elevator, *Carlos* continued patrolling hallways around the suite where the cats and dancing pig were staying, measuring and committing every last detail to memory.

**\* \* \***

*En Los Muelles en Belém*[24]

While the puma was busy in the hotel, his old friend from the Amazon River was doing his own prowling.

*Ramos* paced up and down the wet, moss-covered, rotting wooden planks of the quay in front of the slip where the *Meteoro* was docked. There was a cool breeze, and the air temperature was only seventy degrees Fahrenheit. But the captain was perspiring.

Sweating bullets, so to speak.

His mind was racing. If he went to the authorities and reported his time with *Carlos*, could he still keep the money? Surely he could. But would he be in trouble for waiting so long? He could tell them the puma had threatened to kill him if he went to the police. Would they believe that? After all, he still had the card showing his boat was free of runaway pumas after the police search when *Carlos* so mysteriously disappeared.

Why was he worrying so much? Maybe the big puma

---

24. At the Wharves in *Belém*

was already dead. It's possible he drowned getting off the boat. Cats aren't good swimmers, are they?

On the other hand, if the puma was still alive and *Ramos* went to the police, that might be reason enough for *Carlos* to come after him and do him in. Mightn't it?

*Ramos* was frustrated. When he was growing up, he'd never had trouble making up his mind, or distinguishing right from wrong. This present dilemma was caused by the money, right? What it all boiled down to was the stack of Argentinean *pesos* he had just deposited into his bank account.

He asked himself, So what's the problem? You have the money. *Carlos* willingly gave it to you, even though you didn't have to take him all the way to the Atlantic. And anyway, you didn't even know your passenger's name at the time. Keep the money—and stop the big questions.

Heaving a big sigh, *Ramos* jumped onto the *Meteoro*, went below to his bunk, and fell immediately into a deep sleep.

✳ ✳ ✳

*En El Hotel Libertador, Otra Vez*[25]

Luigi and Luisa skipped down the hallway when the elevator stopped on the twenty-first floor. After both *desayuno y almuerzo de helado*,[26] the twins had a big sugar rush . . . energy to burn. Making them even more hyper was

---

25. At the Hotel *Libertador*, Again
26. Ice cream for breakfast and lunch

the excitement of having their stupendous plan so well received by the grownups.

Dusty had insisted they all return to the hotel while the *capitán y teniente* gathered the equipment they would need, mostly so Luigi and Luisa could take a nap.

Fat chance!

As Cincinnati opened the door to the suite, Luisa stopped dead in her tracks. She licked a front paw and lifted it into the air.

"Wait a minute, everybody," she said urgently. "I smell something in this hallway."

"All hotels have their own smells, Luisa. Quit stalling and come take your nap," Dusty chided.

"No," Luigi said. "I smell it, too. It's for real, Dusty."

Cincinnati seemed to take the twins seriously. "What are you two smelling?" He sniffed the air.

Now Buzzer and Dusty were sniffing, too.

"It's puma," Luisa said. "I smell puma!"

Luigi agreed, eyes wide. "*Carlos* has been here."

*What do you think Luigi and Luisa's plan might be? How are they going to capture* Carlos? *Will* Ramos *be questioned by the authorities? Will he really get to keep all the money? What about the big puma? Will his strange, though not unpleasant, odor give him away? And will Luigi and Luisa get sick from eating so many sweets?*

# Aprendamos a Hablar en Español
by Dusty Louise

Ahora ustedes pueden hablar un poco de Español. Vamos a aprender aún más.[27]

| In English | In Spanish | Say It Like This |
| --- | --- | --- |
| Breakfast | Desayuno | day-say-OO-noh |
| Lunch | Almuerzo | ahl-MWAIR-zoh |
| Dinner | Cena | SAY-nah |
| Snack | Refrigerio | ray-free-HAIR-ee-oh |
| Table | Mesa | MAY-sah |
| Chair | Silla | SEE-zhah |
| Dining room | Comedor | coh-may-DOHR |
| Kitchen | Cocina | co-SEE-nah |
| Plate | Plato | PLAH-toh |
| Cup | Taza | TAHT-zah |
| Glass | Vaso | VAH-szoh |
| Knife | Cuchillo | coo-CHEE-zhoh |
| Fork | Tenedor | ten-ay-DOHR |
| Spoon | Cuchara | coo-CHAR-ah |
| Napkin | Servilleta | sair-vee-ZHET-ah |
| Bowl | Tazón | tah-ZOHN |
| Tablecloth | Mantel | mahn-TELL |

---

27. Now you are able to speak a little Spanish. Let's learn some more.

# * Chapter 13 *
# Visitando a Caperucita Roja[1]

*Carlos Se Está Concentrando*[2]

After the surprise of bumping into *Jaime el botones* near the elevators, *Carlos* knew he had to do some serious soul-searching. How did he miss the obvious scent and human body warmth so close to him?

Back in his room, he thought, I'm out of practice. I'm not ready to take on the *agitadores de Norteamérica*.[3] I have to get out on the streets first and hone my senses—especially my senses of smell and feel.

He made a plan. This afternoon, I'll walk to the *Sheraton del centro*[4] and stand in the shadow of that fountain that saved *el gato blanco y negro*.[5] I'll stand there until I can hear every drop of water as it falls, one drop at a time. Then I'll cross the little park and the big street to *la estación del ferro-*

---

1. Visiting Little Red Riding Hood
2. *Carlos Is Concentrating*
3. troublemakers from North America
4. downtown Sheraton
5. the black and white cat

*carril*[6] and listen to the wheels of the trains on each track, until I can tell without looking which wheel needs more grease. *En el vestíbulo de la estación,*[7] I'll close my eyes and ears until I can tell *el número de pasajeros*[8] by smell alone.

When once again I can hear the squeak of a mouse in the dining car of a passing train, distinguish the big drops of falling water from the smaller drops in the dreaded fountain, and smell the almonds on a child's ice cream cone from across the street, then I'll be ready to catch that pesky cat and his dancing pig friend. Then, and only then. *Carlos* slipped out his door, grabbed his salesman's case, *un paraguas y su impermeable,*[9] and headed for the elevator.

Eyes closed, of course.

The sky was overcast, and *Carlos* sniffed the overpowering smell of ozone in the air. Rain was coming. All the better to test his senses.

* * *

*En el Hotel Otra Vez*[10]

"I believe them," Cincinnati said emphatically, and Buzzer said, "So do I."

Luigi and Luisa looked at Dusty Louise. Was she going to agree with her brother and his friend? Or would she assume that they just were making up wild tales? The two of them had been known to concoct little fantasies in the past.

---

6. the railroad station
7. In the station's lobby,
8. the number of passengers
9. an umbrella and his raincoat
10. In the Hotel Again

But if Buzzer Louis and Cincinnati the dancing pig believed them, well, this story ought to be a slam-dunk as truth.

Finally, Dusty sighed and shook her head as if to clear out cobwebs. Then she smiled at the twins. "Okay, I believe you, too," she said, "and it frightens me. That terrible terrorist is in this very hotel. And on our floor!" She looked around the room. "Do you think he's actually been here while we were at the PFA headquarters?"

Just then *Carlos* passed by their closed door, counting nineteen paces from his room as he made his way to the elevator and then into the streets to sharpen his senses. Luisa sniffed the air. She walked slowly around the parlor, Luigi following. Both kittens went into the two bedrooms and the bathroom, sniffing away. When they came back into the small parlor, Luisa said with conviction, "No, Dusty. *Carlos no estuvo aquí en este cuarto.*"[11]

Luigi agreed. "*Carlos* didn't come in here, and neither did any other puma, for that matter. No pumas in our room, Dusty," he said. "Yet."

"How can you be sure?" Dusty looked nervous.

Luisa cocked her head and batted her eyelashes. "It's simple, Dusty. Pumas smell funny." She pointed to where Dusty had slept the night before, "That bedroom smells like you. And the other one smells like Buzzer and Cincinnati." She nodded to Luigi.

Her tiny orange brother chimed in. "And this little parlor smells like vanilla ice cream and chocolate cake. I wonder why that is?" He winked and Luisa laughed out loud.

---

11. *Carlos* was not here in this room.

Fortunately for the twins, Dusty didn't get the joke.

Still shaken, Dusty looked to Buzzer and Cincinnati. "What do we do now? Luisa and Luigi need a nap, but I'm not sure I want to stay in this room . . . or even in this hotel."

Before Buzzer or Cincinnati could answer, Luigi spoke up. "Look, Dusty, there's no time for naps. That puma is right in this hotel, and we have a lot of work to do!"

"Like scouting out the locations in the plan, Dusty," Luisa said. " We haven't even seen *Los Jardines de Palermo*[12] yet, except on a tourist map. If that's going to be where we capture *Carlos,* we need to see it now."

As if the two of them were speaking in tandem, Luigi added, "We have to know if it's big enough to handle the crowd, but not so big that it'll be too hard to spot *Carlos,* you know."

Luisa chimed in, "Or smell him. I mean, how many pumas can there be in one place at one time in the middle of a big city?"

"Eleven," Luigi answered, to Luisa's delight.

"All right, you two," Dusty said, giving the twins a stern look. "Let's try to be serious here. This is not a game. There's a dangerous international terrorist wandering around right under our noses. Or at least under your noses."

"I'm afraid it *is* a game, Dusty," Cincinnati said, "a serious game with high stakes. Hide-and-seek with a big cat in the city. And we'd better win. Losing is not an option."

Luisa had wandered over toward the door to the hallway.

---

12. the Gardens of Palermo, a park in *Buenos Aires*

"Wait! The scent is even stronger coming under this door. *Carlos* may be in the hall right now!"

She started to open the door, but Buzzer grabbed her and put one front paw over her mouth, whispering, "Shhh."

Slowly he turned the doorknob and opened the door a crack, peeping out.

Suddenly they heard the ding of an elevator arriving at their floor. Then the elevator doors opened, and closed.

Luigi, pressed up against the crack in the door and sniffed. "*Carlos* either just got on the elevator, or he just got off. He's either just coming, or he's just going. Am I right, Luisa?"

"No doubt about it, *hermanito*.[13] The scent's almost over-powering. I'd say he just passed by this door and got on that elevator. For the moment, at least, he's gone."

"Let's check it out," Luigi said, squeezing through the crack in the door and bounding into the hallway.

Before Buzzer could stop her, Luisa shot out the door behind him. The two of them sniffed their way straight toward the elevators.

Cincinnati flung the door open, and he and Buzzer raced toward the twins and the elevator.

Dusty peeped around the door from inside the room.

* * *

*Frente a la Fuente de Agua*[14]

Meanwhile, *Carlos* stood quietly in a light rain next to

13. little brother
14. In Front of the Fountain

the fountain in front of the *Hotel Sheraton del Centro*, the place which, by chance and because of Buzzer's tears from that night, had resulted in the *Norteamericanos* and *Carlos* staying at the same nearby hotel.

The big puma, in his rocking horse salesman disguise, held his blue and white striped *paraguas* low over his head as the gentle rain fell. The fountain was running full blast beside him, torrents of water under high pressure rising and falling in a million droplets a minute into the big oval-shaped pool at its base.

*Carlos*, his eyes closed and his nose packed with cotton balls— to block out both his sight and his sense of smell, looked almost in a trance. He was concentrating with an intensity rare, if not unique, among pumas as well as humans. First, he had mastered separating the sound of the rain falling on his umbrella from the sound of the water in the fountain. Then he began to isolate the sounds of the raindrops dripping off his umbrella and hitting *la acera de abajo*[15] from the splash of droplets bouncing off the pool's surface and out onto the *acera*. Yes, he was getting back the sharpness that had dulled during his four years in prison.

Satisfied at the progress he had made, *Carlos* took a leisurely stoll across the little park and the big avenue and

---

15. the sidewalk below

made his way to the train station. Once inside, he would re-move the cotton from his nostrils and put new cotton into his ears. Then he would spend an hour or so sharpening his sense of smell in an atmosphere rich with smells—of wet passengers boarding trains, of dry passengers coming off the trains, and of the cafés serving a variety of foods and drinks—both bland and aromatic.

* * *

*En El Bote Meteoro en Belém*

*Capitan Ramos* slept soundly. He was dreaming pleasant dreams about what he could do with all the money *Carlos* the Puma had paid him, money that was now safely in his bank account. Perhaps he would spend some of it on a new paint job for the *Meteoro*. He could have his diesel engine overhauled, and he could remodel and improve his cabin below decks. He might even add an amplifier and fine speakers for an audio system, allowing beautiful music to diminish the boredom of his long trips up and down the river. Or just to entertain a young lady he had recently met at a bar near the wharves in *Belém,* a girl from *Ipanema,* the beautiful beach in *Río de Janeiro.*

*Ramos* was smiling at a vision of that girl as a pounding on the upstairs door to his cabin suddenly awakened him. He heard voices, loud voices. Shaking off sleep, he suddenly heard the voices become clear.

"¡Capitán Ramos, abra la puerta. Es la policía!"[16]

They were speaking Spanish, not the usual Portuguese

16. "Captain Ramos, open the door. Police here!"

of *Brasil*. *Ramos* knew that meant they knew him, and knew that he was Argentinean and spoke Spanish better than Portuguese.

So the authorities were here after all. Although he didn't recognize the voices, he thought it good that they likely would be officials he knew. He thought hurriedly, I have always kept my nose clean. I've run an honest business. Nobody would assume I've done anything wrong. I'd better see what they want. But I won't say a word about the money.

*Ramos* shouted back between the pounding and the shouting voices, "*Voy en un momento. Estaba durmiendo. Un momento, por favor.*"[17]

He climbed the short stairs and opened the door. Seeing the same two officers who had searched the *Meteoro* on the Amazon River two nights ago, he almost heaved a big sigh of relief, but caught himself just in time.

"*Buenos tardes, agentes,*" *Ramos* said, forcing a smile. *¿Por qué están aquí hoy?*[18]

"We're still looking for an escaped criminal. And we want to talk to everyone who traveled up and down the big river in the last few days. Come on out on deck, *Capitán*. Sorry to wake you. We'll only take a minute or two of your time," the taller officer said, and added "Have you ever heard of that international terrorist known as *Carlos* the Puma?"

Before *Ramos* could answer, the shorter, pudgier of the two policemen added, "Better yet, did you see him along the river anywhere?"

17. "I'll be there in a minute. I was sleeping. A minute, please."
18. "Good afternoon, officers. Why are you here today?"

# * *Visitando a Caperucita Roja* *

*Ramos* gulped. It was decision time for him.

* * *

*En la Suite del Hotel Sheraton Libertador*

Back in their suite after confirming via the little twins' noses that *Carlos,* or at least a puma, had recently walked past their door and gotten into an elevator, Luigi and Luisa were anxious to get on with their part of their stupendous plan.

"*Es hora de visitar a Caperucita Roja,*"[19] Luisa said, looking at Dusty as if to say, "See, Miss Smarty, I can speak Spanish, too."

Dusty, Buzzer and Cincinnati looked confused. Only Luigi seemed to understand his sister's strange comment.

"Little Red Riding Hood?" Dusty answered. "What in the world are you talking about, Luisa? Do you want me to read you a story before you take a nap, or what?"

Luisa looked insulted. She turned to Luigi in exasperation. "You explain it, Luigi. We're far ahead of everybody else in this room, I think."

Luigi stood, puffed out his chest and folded his front paws in front of it. He was going into his televangelist routine, Luisa thought, and probably just in time.

"You see, my friends," Luigi began, pacing back and forth and doing his best to look confident, "it's like this. *Los Jardines de Palermo* is a park not too far from here. In Luisa's and my plan, that park is what we in the business like to call 'ground zero.' It's the place where we expect to wrap up that smelly puma once and for all."

---

19. "It's time to visit Little Red Riding Hood"

Luigi paused and postured some more as Luisa looked on, barely able to keep from laughing.

The little kitten resumed his monologue. "Right smack in that park is a nifty statue, a cool piece of art created by a Frenchman, I'm surprised to admit. And that statue is of none other than . . ." Here Luigi paused and pointed to Luisa, who took the cue.

"Little Red Riding Hood," she almost shouted. "Known around these parts as '*Caperucita Roja.*' It's time to pay our respects to our new best friend in Argentina, except for *Capitán Paloma* and *Teniente* Chuck, of course, and that new best friend is . . . *Caperucita Roja*! *Vámonos al parque, equipo.*"[20]

Cincinnati applauded the twins' mini-drama. He turned to Buzzer and whispered, "These two are sure wired tight today, Buzz."

Buzzer whispered back, "If I didn't know better, Cincinnati, I'd think they've been eating candy all night. Seems like too much sugar to me."

*How do you think Ramos will answer the policemen's questions? Will he tell the truth? Or will he play games with them? And what about Carlos? Is he getting his super keen senses and awareness back? How can he get them back so fast? When do you think the sugar will work its way out of Luigi and Luisa's systems so they won't be quite so hyper? What about the kittens' stupendous plan? Do you have any idea how it might work?*

20. Let's go to the park, team.

# Aprendamos a Hablar en Español
## by Luigi and Luisa

*Hola. Somos los dos gatitos gemelos. Esta vez no es Dusty Louise. Ahora, para ustedes, aquí están los nombres de algunos tipos de helado. Mmmm.*[21]

| In English | In Spanish | Say It Like This |
| --- | --- | --- |
| Vanilla | Vainilla | vy-ah-NEE-zhah |
| Chocolate | Chocolate | Choh-coh-LAH-teh |
| Dulce de leche<br>Does not translate to English | Dulce de leche | DOOL-seh day LAY-cheh |
| Strawberry | Fresa | FRAY-sah |
| Raspberry | Frambuesa | frahm-BWAY-sah |
| Peach | Durazno | doo-RAHZ-noh |
| Pistachio | Pistacho | pees-TAH-choh |
| Caramel | Caramelo | cahr-ah-MAY-loh |
| Coffee | Café | cah-FAY |
| Toffee | Caramelo | cahr-ah-MAY-loh |
| Cherry | Cereza | say-RAY-szah |
| Banana | Banana | bah-NAH-nah |
| Peanut butter | Mantequilla de cacahuate | mahn-tay-KEE-zhah day cah-cah-HWAT-the |
| Sardine[22] | Sardina | sahr-DEE-nah |

21. Hello. We are the two kitten twins here. It's not Dusty Louise this time. Now, for you, here are the names of some kinds of ice cream. Mmmm.
22. Luigi's favorite flavor

# * Chapter 14 *
# Planeando el Trabajo.
# Y Trabajando el Plan.[1]

*En el Bote Meteoro en Belém*

*Ramos* took a deep breath. *Los dos policía* had asked him a direct question about *Carlos* the Puma. Had he seen the big cat on his trip down *el Río Amazonas*?

The *capitán* looked the shorter of the policemen straight in the eye.

"*No, señor,*" he said convincingly, "*Yo no pude ver nada en el río. Había mucha niebla. No vi al puma. Lo siento.*"[2]

The two policemen looked at one another. Did they believe *Ramos*, or were they thinking he'd lied to them?

"*Gracias, capitán,*" the taller policeman said. "*Si usted ve al puma, llámenos inmediatamente, por favor.*"[3] He handed *Ramos* a business card.

---

1. Planning the Work. And Working the Plan.
2. "No, sir. I couldn't see anything along the river. There was a lot of fog. I didn't see the puma. I'm sorry."
3. "Thank you, captain. If you see the puma, call us at once, please."

With that, the policemen turned, stepped up onto the slippery wooden planks of the wharf and walked away.

Did they believe me? *Ramos* wondered. He quickly decided that his back-up story would be that *Carlos* threatened to kill him if he talked to the authorities. That'll work, he told himself. *Sí. Es una buena historia.*[4]

Still, *Ramos* wondered if they would be back. And if so, when.

✳ ✳ ✳

*En el Hotel Sheraton Libertador*

"Hurry up in there, you two," Dusty called from the parlor into the bathroom. "We're ready to go to that *Jardínes de Palermo,* or wherever you said that statue is—'ground zero.'"

Luisa had never seen Luigi look so distressed. He wore a sad expression, as if he'd just dropped a brand new ice cream cone in the dirt.

"Give it up, Luigi," his little twin coaxed him. "It's obvious by now, or should be. Bart was just lying, as usual."

Flushing the toilet for the fifteenth time, Luigi peered into the bowl and shook his head. "Why would he do that, Luisa?" he asked. "This water's going the same way around that it does at home. I don't understand."

"You need some better scientific sources than Bart Simpson, Luigi," Luisa said, hoping to bring her *hermanito* out of his trance. "Besides, who cares? We need to get to *la estatua de Caperucita Roja en Los Jardines de Palermo*[5]—'ground

---

4. "Yes. That's a good story."
5. the statue of Little Red Riding Hood in the Gardens of Palermo

zero' for our stupendous plan.Leave the toilet alone, and let's go!"

Luigi trudged back into the parlor, his mood changing from morose to excited in the six steps it took him to get there. "*Vámonos,*"[6] he said, coming back to life instantly, as only Luigi seemed able to do. "Please call Chuck and *la capitán,*" he said to Cincinnati. "Ask them to meet us *en la estatua en treinta minutos.*"[7]

*       *       *

*En el Vestíbulo del Hotel Sheraton Libertador*[8]

*Carlos* sat sipping a Coca Cola Zero in *el Bar Maximiliano* next to the lobby of the hotel. Still disguised as a rocking horse salesman, he peeped from behind a copy of *La Nación, Buenos Aires'* daily newspaper. He wasn't really reading it so much as he was using it to keep those coming into and out of the lobby from seeing his face.

As he looked across the passageway toward the registration desk, an elevator door opened and out stepped Buzzer, Cincinnati, Dusty and the little twins. They headed straight for the circular drive where the bell captain would call a cab to take them to see *Caperucita Roja.*

*Carlos* shifted in his seat and leaned toward *la puerta giradora*[9] that led outside. He wanted to hear where they were headed, and he was only five or six meters from the door. With his hearing now finely honed, he thought he

---

6. "Let's go!"
7. at the statue in thirty minutes
8. In the Hotel Sheraton Libertador Lobby
9. the revolving door

should be able to hear them tell the bell captain where they wanted to go.

Just as Cincinnati turned to the bell captain and began to speak, *un pianista*[10] launched into a stylized, and far too loud, version of "Misty" on the grand piano near the little round table where *Carlos* sat.

"*¡Caramba!*" *Carlos* said. The piano drowned out Cincinnati's voice so the puma couldn't hear where the group was going. "*Tal vez mis orejotas aún no están listas.*"[11]

*Carlos* had thought he had his hearing finely tuned. But that dratted pianista had shown him clearly that he could still be confused, especially by unexpected sounds. And what other kinds of sounds even count in my business? he asked himself. *¡Nada!*

As *Carlos* considered how badly he had handled the surprise of the piano's cranking up, *el botones Jaime* wandered through *la puerta giradora* and sidled up to *Carlos'* table. He leaned down and spoke softly into the puma's ear, "They have gone to the Gardens of Palermo, *Señor Vendedor. Tal vez son turistas solamente.*"[12]

*Carlos* smiled at the news *Jaime* brought. "*No lo creo, Señor Botones. Son detectives. ¿Pero, porqué van a los jardines?*"[13] *Carlos* wondered aloud.

*Jaime* shrugged. "*No sé,*"[14] he added as an afterthought,

---

10. a pianist
11. "Maybe my big ears are not ready yet."
12. Mister Salesman. Maybe they're just tourists.
13. "I don't believe so, Mister Bellman. They are detectives. But why are they going to the gardens?"
14. "I don't know."

holding out his hand. *Carlos* put twenty *pesos* into the bell-man's open palm and said, *"Buen trabajo, Jaime."*[15]

Then the big puma stood, left *otros diez pesos en la mesa para pagar por su*[16] Coca Cola Zero, and headed for the elevators and his junior suite on the 21st floor. He had work to do. First, though, he had a lot of thinking to do.

✴ ✴ ✴

*En Los Jardines de Palermo*

"Look at her, Luisa!" Luigi said. "She must be six or seven feet tall, and white all over."

---

15. "Good work, Jaime."
16. . . . another ten pesos on the table to pay for his Coca Cola Zero

Luisa added, "Wouldn't you think she might have a red cape, Luigi? I think it's strange that Little Red Riding Hood is all white."

"That's what happens when you turn a Frenchman loose to create art, Luisa," said Luigi. *"En Francia, tal vez la roja es la blanca. ¿Qué piensas?"* [17]

"This place ought to work fine," Cincinnati said to Buzzer and Dusty. "If we can get the *PFA* to block off *Avenida Sarmiento,* [18] we can set the Bell Jet Ranger down right there in the middle of the street. And there's plenty of room straight across there"—he pointed north across the wide avenue—"to mark off the lines and set up some big bleachers. Yes, I think this will work just fine." Buzzer and Dusty nodded in agreement as *Teniente* Chuck and *Capitán Paloma* pulled up to the curb in Chuck's dark blue Fiat cruiser.

Luigi and Luisa joined the group that was gathered next to a sidewalk concession stand. Luigi spoke up. "This place is just great. So far, the plan's falling into place perfectly."

Luisa turned to the *capitán.* "Have you cleared the event with the Pink House—*La Casa Rosada*—yet?" she asked.

*Capitán Paloma* answered, "*Sí,* Luisa. *Todo está perfecto.* [19] We're all set to make the announcement tonight. It will create quite a stir, I'm sure. Have you seen all you need to see here? If you have, we need to get back to our offices so you can meet another member of the team—someone you

---

17. "In France, maybe red is white, do you think?"
18. Sarmiento Avenue (the street that runs in front of the statue of *Caperucita Roja*)
19. "Yes, Luisa. Everything's perfect.

may have seen doing other things. But someone who will be, how do you say, 'indispensable?'"

Dusty answered, "Yes, *capitán*. 'Indispensable' is the right word, I think."

"*Bueno*, Dusty," the captain said. "Now let's go to our headquarters to complete the afternoon's work. Perhaps you would care to see a tango show tonight?"

Buzzer answered, "Let's save the tango for the evening after *Carlos* is all wrapped up and in your *cárcel*,[20] *Capitán*."

Everyone squeezed into Chuck's Fiat for the ten-minute ride to the headquarters of *PFA, Policía Federal de Argentina*.

✳ ✳ ✳

*En Belém, Otra Vez*[21]

*Ramos* made a decision. Spur of the moment though it was, he decided to make himself and the *Meteoro* scarce. So he backed the trawler from its berth and headed south-east—and then south to Argentina. If the *policía* really wanted to talk to him any time soon, he thought it best not to be easily found. He would drift down the Atlantic coast to the mouth of *Río de la Plata*[22], east of *Buenos Aires*. There he'd find a quiet berth and tie up while monitoring the news of the search for *Carlos* the Puma. If the big cat were captured before *Ramos* had to talk to anybody again, so much the better.

His usual mail run up the big river could wait until the smoke cleared.

—————
20. jail
21. In Belém, Again
22. Silver River

* * *

*En la Oficina de PFA*

On their first visit to PFA headquarters, Luigi and Luisa had been so excited at the prospect of presenting their stupendous plan that they hadn't noticed it was so beautiful.

"This is one of the prettiest buildings I've seen here in *Buenos Aires*, Luigi," Luisa commented as Chuck stopped in front and backed into what must have been a reserved parking space. "It's all yellow and white and looks like it was just built yesterday, but Chuck said it was more than a hundred years old. I hope I look this good when I'm a hundred."

Luigi laughed. "I like the big courtyard inside, Luisa. Who's that statue of, anyway?" Luigi shifted topics in his own brand of jump-speak.

"I think it's the guy who started all this police business here in Argentina. *Don Marcos Paz.* I wonder whether he was a good guy."

"I don't know, Luisa. He looks really old, though," said Luigi.

As the team walked up the stairs to the soundproof interrogation room where they had met earlier, a familiar yet unknown man joined them.

"I've seen him before, Luisa," Luigi offered. "Maybe when we were here last time, do you think?"

"No, Luigi, I think I've seen him at our hotel. I'm sure that's where I've seen him. But he wasn't dressed the same. I'm sure his clothes were different."

"How?" Luisa thought about this, closing her eyes and

concentrating. Then her eyes popped open, and she said so only Luigi could hear, "*Él es un botones* at our hotel, Luigi—a bellman."

Now Luigi remembered, too. "Or maybe he's a twin, Luisa," he offered.

Back in the soundproof interrogation room, as everyone started to take a seat, Chuck introduced the new member of the group. "I want to introduce all of you to our secret, undercover—Is that the right word, Dusty?—agent who is working with us as a bellman at your hotel. Dusty, Buzzer, Cincinnati, Luigi, Luisa, meet detective sergeant *Jaime Espinosa* of the *PFA*."

Dusty nodded, to indicate that "undercover" was precisely the right word.

Chuck continued, "*Jaime*, would you please tell our *amigos* from North America what you're doing in the hotel? Thanks."

*Jaime* rose. He looked at the group and smiled. Speaking slowly, he said, "I'm working for *Carlos* the Puma."

At that, Buzzer shot forward in his chair. Cincinnati leapt up, clapped his front hooves together and smiled the biggest smile the twins had ever seen on his face.

Luigi spoke first. "You're spying on *Carlos* for us?" he asked.

"Not spying exactly, Luigi," *Jaime* answered. "What I'm doing is more like reporting on your activities—when you leave, when you come back, even where you're going."

"Why would you do that?" Luisa wanted to know.

"So that I can gain his trust quickly, Luisa. *La capitán* and Chuck have told me of your stupendous plan, and I think maybe I can lure *Carlos* right to where you want him, if I can gain his trust. Don't worry, I won't tell him anything that will lead to harm for you or any of the rest of us."

"But as I understand your plan, you're going to need a totally impartial referee who is fluent in both Spanish and Portuguese, *¿verdad?*"

"Right you are, *Jaime*," Luigi answered. "That's one loose end we haven't tied up yet. Whom do you have in mind for that job?"

*Jaime* smiled. He looked slowly around the room, and then he answered, "None other than your friend and mine—*Carlos* the Puma!"

The twins looked at one another.

Then, together, they saluted *Jaime* with four dewclaws up.

"Even better!" Luigi almost shouted.

"Just perfect!" Luisa added. "Better than what we had in our stupendous plan, eh, Luigi?"

"*Sí, sí*," Luigi answered. "*Mucho mejor.*"[23]

*Why do you think* Ramos *is heading toward* Buenos Aires? *There are plenty of places he could hide out without traveling so far, aren't there? Do you think there's any good reason that* Caperucita Roja's *statue is all white? Will* Jaime *be able to keep on fooling* Carlos *and earn his trust? And what in the world was he talking about when he said that* Carlos *could be 'the referee?' Why does the referee, whatever that means, need to be able to speak both Spanish and Portuguese?*

---

23. "Yes, yes. Much better."

# Aprendamos a Hablar en Español
by Dusty Louise

*Tal vez, el gran plan de Luigi y Luisa incluye deportes. Si es verdad, aquí están algunos nombres de deportes.*[24]

| In English | In Spanish | Say It Like This |
| --- | --- | --- |
| Baseball | Béisbol | BAYS-bohl |
| Basketball | Baloncesto | bahl-ohn-SESS-toh |
| Cycling | Ciclismo | see-CLEES-moh |
| Auto racing | Carreras de coches | car-REHR-ahs day COH-chez |
| Skiing | Esquí | ess-KEE |
| Football | Fútbol americano | FOOHT-bohl ah-mehr-ee-CAH-noh |
| Gymnastics | Gimnasio | heem-NAH-see-oh |
| Hockey | Hockey | OH-kee |
| Running | Carrera | cah-REHR-rah |
| Sailing | Vela | VAY-lah |
| Soccer | Fútbol | FOOHT-bohl |
| Swimming | Natación | nah-tah-see-OHN |
| Tennis | Tenis | TEH-nees |
| Volleyball | Voleibol | VOH-lay-ee-bohl |
| Golf | Golf | GOALF |

---

24. Perhaps Luigi and Luisa's big plan involves sports. If that's true, here are some names of sports.

# * Chapter 15 *

# La Copa de Caperucita Roja:
# Un Juego Gigante Para Los
# Gatitos de Kindergarten[1]

*En la Pequeña Suite de Carlos*[2]

*Carlos* reached into his fanny pack to pull out another twenty pesos as *Jaime, el botones y agente secreto,*[3] reported in.

"What have you learned this afternoon, *Jaime?*" *Carlos* asked, expecting another update on the four Texas cats and the dancing pig.

"They've not returned yet from *Los Jardines de Palermo, señor,*" *Jaime* answered. "It has now been *tres horas y media*[4] since they left in a taxi. But I'll keep watching, *señor*. It'll soon be dark, and I don't think they'll want to be in the

---

1. The Little Red Riding Hood Cup: A Giant Game for Kindergarten Kittens
2. In *Carlos'* Small Suite
3. *Jaime,* the bellman and secret agent
4. Three-and-a-half hours

park too late. *Durante el invierno la noche es fría en el jardín.*[5] But there is bigger news afoot. If the rumors I heard in the lobby a few minutes ago are true, you will perhaps have a perfect chance to capture the big cat and the pig. If you are disguised, of course."

*Carlos* bolted from the bed. *"¡Dígame los rumores inmediatamente, Jaime!"*[6] the big cat shouted. *"¿Qué pasó?"*[7]

★ ★ ★

*Cerca de la Boca del Río de La Plata*[8]

*Ramos* steered the *Meteoro* from the salt water of the South Atlantic into the current of the freshwater known as the *Río de La Plata*. Soon he could see neither bank as he chugged slowly upstream. He told himself, This is the widest river in the world. Two-hundred twenty-five kilometers wide, or one hundred thirty-seven miles.

Even though he had grown up in *Buenos Aires* and been around boats and water all his life, he had never understood the big river's name. It's called "Silver," he thought, but it's not silver. *Es marrón. Marrón completamente.*[9]

In school, he had been taught that the color of the river comes from sand and silt boiling in the fast current—sand and silt that's been dredged and used for hundreds of years in construction, as *Buenos Aires* grew from a small community to one of the biggest cities anywhere.

---

5. It's very chilly at night in the garden in winter.
6. "Tell me the rumors immediately, *Jaime!*"
7. "What's happening?"
8. Near the Mouth of the *Río de La Plata*
9. It's brown. Completely brown.

But his mind was wandering. *Ramos* needed to concentrate, to keep a sharp lookout for water patrols of the *PFA*, just in case the authorities had decided they wanted to talk to him again. He would move farther toward the big city, sixty-five miles—one hundred kilometers—inland, and tie up at an out-of-the-way place. There he could listen to the news and follow the progress of the search for *Carlos*.

As he steered the *Meteoro* upstream, his mind began to wander again. Whatever happens, the money is mine. It's mine, and I'll never say a word about it!

His thoughts preoccupied with the money, he missed the approach of a *PFA* boat.

* * *

*En la Oficina del PFA Otra Vez*[10]

*Jaime* had left the meeting an hour ago, to return to the hotel and keep working to get *Carlos* to trust him.

The rest of the group was concentrating on the tactical details of Luigi and Luisa's stupendous plan. At the moment, Cincinnati was speaking. "When will the announcement be made, again, and who will actually make it?" he asked *la capitán*.

"The news will come from the Pink House—*La Casa Rosada*. The Argentinean executive offices, similar to your White House," *Capitán Paloma* answered, and added, "It is of such great importance that the president will make the announcement in person. She will speak to the people

---

10. At the *PFA* Office Again

and the media from the same balcony where *Evita y Juan Perón*[11] often delivered important messages more than fifty years ago. It will be big news, *señor*. You may be sure of that. When the president goes out on that balcony to talk to the people, our world comes to a complete stop." She smiled at Cincinnati.

Luigi turned to Chuck. "Do we have all the equipment and materials on the list Luisa and I gave you?"

Chuck pulled a notepad from his pocket and scanned the list he had written in their earlier meeting.

"Almost everything, Luigi," he answered. "We have what you might call a 'souped-up' old car, a twenty-five-year-old Peugeot It has a red hood, green front fenders and a white body. *Tres colores—rojo, verde y blanco.*[12] It looks like a wreck, but it has a Mercedes-Benz engine and gears, and it will go very fast. We use it for *el trabajo clandestine.*"[13] Again Chuck consulted his list. "We also have an almost new Bell Jet Ranger, Cincinnati, for you and Dusty to use. To hide its identity, you will take off from the helipad on top of a big hospital, disguised as a television crew. Do you need to see the chopper before flying it?"

"*No es necesario,*[14] Chuck," Cincinnati answered. "I'm cleared to fly almost any Bell whirlybird."

---

11. *General Juan Perón* was elected president of Argentina several times. His wife, *Eva Duarte*—known affectionately as *Evita* (Little Eva), was a young peasant girl from the *pampas*, Argentina's vast grasslands. *Evita* remains a national heroine to many, although she died of cancer in 1953 at the age of thirty-three.
12. Three colors—red, green and white
13. undercover work
14. "That's not necessary, Chuck."

"*Bueno*,"[15] Chuck said, and turned to Luigi and Luisa. "Luisa and Luigi, I have the skateboards, scissors, tweezers, two disguises, and a hand-held stun gun in my office. I think that's everything you need, except two Vespas."

To *Capitán Paloma* he asked, "Have you located the Vespas yet?"

*Capitán Paloma* shook her head. "Not yet, *teniente. No hay muchas Vespas aquí en Buenos Aires. Hay muchas motocicletas, pero no Vespas.*"[16]

She added, "I have several people looking, but I'm not sure if we will find them in time." Turning to Luisa, she asked, "How important are the Vespas to the tactics of your plan, Luisa?"

---

15. "Good."
16. There are not many Vespas here in *Buenos Aires*. There are many motorcycles, but no Vespas.

Luisa looked inquiringly at Luigi, who shrugged as if to say, "It's your call, little sister."

Then Luisa confessed, "*Capitán*, the Vespas are not critical."

She glanced at Luigi, who nodded in agreement.

Luisa went on, "In fact they have nothing to do with the plan to capture *Carlos*. Nothing at all, really. You see, *Capitán*, Luigi and I just love to ride Vespas. We thought after *Carlos* was captured, we might race around the park. Know what I mean?"

Luisa looked around the room, her confession complete.

Buzzer, Cincinnati, and Chuck burst out laughing. Dusty, though, was embarrassed beyond words. She simply got up and left the room in shame.

When he got his laughter under control, Chuck asked Luisa, "Is there anything else on the list that we don't really need, Luisa?"

Luigi seized the moment to take a bit of the pressure off his *hermanita*. "Skateboards, Chuck. We don't have any use for skateboards at the event, but there's a big parking garage under our hotel, a garage with steep ramps. Luisa and I thought we could teach Dusty and Cincinnati to ride down those ramps very, very fast." He looked at his *compadres*. "So I guess you can send the skateboards back. And forget the Vespas."

Chuck smiled. "I think we can find a way to keep the skateboards, you two. I might even join you on those ramps. It sounds like fun to me, and when we wrap up that puma, we should have some fun, *¿Verdad?*"

# * La Copa de Caperucita Roja *

## * * *

*En el Río de La Plata Otra Vez*[17]

The Argentine *PFA* cigarette boat was almost alongside the *Meteoro* before *Ramos* snapped out of his daydream about the money.

"*Hola, capitán*," one of the *policía* called out, as *Ramos* pulled back on the throttle and slipped his trawler out of gear. "I see that your boat has *Brasileño* registration." He pointed to a series of letters and numbers on the bow of the *Meteoro*. "So what are you doing in Argentine waters, *señor*? May we see your passport, *por favor*?"[18]

*Ramos* handed his passport across, as the cigarette boat nudged gently against his trawler.

"Ah, I see you are *un Argentino*,"[19] the policeman said. Again he asked, "Why do you come to *Buenos Aires*?"

"I'm taking a small vacation, coming back to my home city for a visit."

"*Bueno. Gracias, señor*,"[20] the policeman said. He handed the passport to another policeman who opened it, swiped one edge against an electronic reader, and reached over to return the captain's passport.

"Enjoy your visit, *capitán*," the second policeman said, smiling.

And the cigarette boat with the two policemen pulled away and accelerated up the river.

*Ramos* heaved a sigh of relief. The whole encounter was

---

17. On the Silver River Again
18. please
19. an Argentinean
20. "Good. Thank you, sir."

just a routine immigration check. Nobody was looking for him. Yet, anyway.

But the captain knew he had made a big mistake. Now that his passport had been swiped across the electronic reader, the authorities in Argentina—and everywhere else, for that matter—would know where he was.

So much for staying invisible for a while, *Ramos* thought, shaking his head and frowning.

He reached up to his radio and tuned in a *Buenos Aires* station just in time to hear a live announcement from the Argentine president . . . delivered from the balcony of *La Casa Rosada*—the Pink House.

✳ ✳ ✳

*En el Bar Maximiliano en el Vestíbulo del Hotel Sheraton Libertador*[21]

*Carlos* sat sipping another Coca Cola Zero, again in disguise and hiding his face with a copy of *Time*, the South American edition.

He sat as far from the big grand piano as he could, although the *pianista* had not arrived yet for his late afternoon set.

*Carlos* was used to getting his way, and he was not happy that *Jaime* had refused to tell him about the rumors the bellman claimed to have overheard. Instead, *Jaime* had suggested that *Carlos* meet him in the lobby bar at nineteen hundred hours—7:00 P.M.

It was now *seis cincuenta y cinco por la noche.*[22] *Carlos*

---

21. In the Maximilian Bar in the Lobby of the Hotel Sheraton Libertador
22. 6:55 in the evening

looked around impatiently for *Jaime*. True, the bellman wasn't late yet, but the puma had been stewing for several hours now, waiting for *Jaime* to divulge the rumors. If something was about to happen that would help *Carlos* get even with that dratted black-and-white cat and his twinkle-toed pig friend, the puma wanted to know about it.

Right now.

*Carlos* was beginning to seethe, and just then *Jaime* stepped out from behind the bar itself and quietly motioned the puma to walk across to the raised platform, where the bellman stood under a big-screen television.

As *Carlos* took the three steps up to the bar level, *Jaime* whispered, "Sit down here for ten minutes, *señor*. Watch and listen to this television. I believe you'll see and hear the big announcement I spoke of earlier."

Turning to leave, *Jaime* added, "I'll meet you in your suite in one hour, *señor*. By then I will have made some contacts I think will help put you right in front of the cat and the pig you seem so interested in."

Handing *Jaime* another twenty *pesos*, *Carlos* spoke to the bellman's back as he walked away. "I'd rather be put right behind those two."

The puma smirked as the evening news began.

* * *

*En la Plaza de Mayo, Enfrente de La Casa Rosada*[23]

Luigi and Luisa peeped out the window from inside *La Casa Rosada* to see the balcony where the president of

---

23. In the Plaza of May, In Front of the Pink House

Argentina was about to appear. They already knew what she was going to say. But the huge crowd of more than 50,000 standing on *La Plaza de Mayo* below didn't. Nor did the half-dozen television crews from CNN, the BBC and local stations.

Electricity was in the air.

Big Klieg lights flashed on outside the balcony.

The president, dressed in a light blue business suit with a white blouse and a yellow bow at her neckline—the precise colors of the Argentinean flag—stepped up to the pack of microphones. She gazed down on the gathered crowd, raised both her arms straight up and waved to the throngs below.

A huge roar went up from the crowd. But it quickly died down when the president leaned into the microphones, signaling she was ready to make an announcement.

As quiet swept over the crowd, she began to speak.

*"Buenas tardes, amigos."*[24] I am very excited to announce a new event that will take place *pasado mañana*[25] right here in *Buenos Aires."* She paused, then asked, "Which country do you think plays the best *fútbol,*[26] *¿Brasil o Argentina?"*

The roar from the crowd was as expected, *"¡Argentina, Argentina, Argentina!"*

She raised her hands to quiet the people, then asked, *"¿De dónde son los gatitos más hábiles, de Brasil o de Argentina?"*[27]

---

24. "Good afternoon, friends."
25. the day after tomorrow
26. soccer
27. "Whose kittens are the most skilled, Brazil's or Argentina's?

Again the roar went up: "*¡Argentina, Argentina, Argentina!*"

The president smiled and waved, and then she made the big announcement. "*Pasado mañana en Los Jardines de Palermo, un equipo de gatitos desde Brasil y un equipo de gatitos de Argentina*[28] will meet to play the first ever 'Little Red Riding Hood Cup.' It will be a huge event for the people of our two countries."

As the applause quieted, she added, "May the best team win. And that will be, most certainly . . . Argentina."

With that, the president left the microphone and retreated into her offices in *La Casa Rosada.*

*How do you think Jaime will try to get Carlos involved in the first-ever Copa de Caperucita Roja? And how have Luisa and Luigi planned to capture the puma at a soccer match? Will Cincinnati and Dusty be able to land a helicopter in the middle of the avenue in front of the statue of Little Red Riding Hood? Why would they even want to do that? What about Chuck? Will he be able to ride a skateboard down the parking garage ramps without breaking a leg? Will Dusty even try?*

28. "Day after tomorrow in the Gardens of Palermo, a team of kittens from Brazil and a team of kittens from Argentina

# Aprendamos a Hablar en Español
by Dusty Louise

¿Cómo se llama en Español? Aquí están algunos nombres de personas en Español.[29]

| In English | In Spanish | Say It Like This |
| --- | --- | --- |
| James | Jaime, or Diego | HY-mee, dee-AY-goh |
| George | Jorge | HOHR-hay |
| Robert | Roberto | ro-BEHR-toh |
| Charles | Carlos | CAHR-lohs |
| Christopher | Cristóbal | krees-TOH-bahl |
| David | David | dah-VEED |
| Donald | Donaldo | doh-NAHL-doh |
| Edward | Eduardo | ay-DWAHR-doh |
| Frank | Paco, or Pancho | PAH-coh, PAHN-choh |
| Henry | Enrique | ehn-REE-keh |
| Joseph | José | hoh-SAY |
| Joe | Pepe | PEH-peh |
| Matthew | Mateo | mah-TAY-oh |
| Peter | Pedro | PED-roh |
| Thomas | Tomás | toh-MAHS |
| Luigi | Luís | loo-EESZ |
| William | Guillermo | gwee-YAIR-moh |
| Ann | Ana | AH-nah |
| Barbara | Barbara | BAHR-bah-rah |
| Kathleen | Catalina | cah-tah-LEE-nah |
| Deborah | Débora | DAY-boh-rah |

29. What is your name in Spanish? Here are some peoples' names in Spanish.

## * La Copa de Caperucita Roja *

| | | |
|---|---|---|
| Elaine | *Elena* | ay-LAY-nah |
| Hope | *Esperanza* | ehs-peh-RAHN-szah |
| Frances | *Francisca* | frahn-SEES-cah |
| Elizabeth | *Isabel* | ee-sah-BELL |
| Linda | *Linda* | LEEN-dah |
| Louise | *Luisa* | loo-EE-sah |
| Margaret | *Margarita* | mahr-gah-REE-tah |
| Martha | *Marta* | MAHR-tah |
| Mary | *María* | mah-REE-ah |
| Rose | *Rosa* | ROH-sah |
| Sarah | *Sara* | SAH-rah |
| Susan | *Susana* | soo-SAH-nah |
| Sophia | *Sofía* | soh-FEE-ah |

# * Chapter 16 *
# Un Agente Secreto Con Integridad[1]

*A las Ocho de la Noche*[2]

*Jaime* stepped confidently into *Carlos'* small suite. He had a smile on his face and looked excited.

"*Señor Vendedor*," he said, "do you still wish to get close to the black-and-white cat and his pig friend? Close to them in a place where you can move and act quickly, and then simply disappear into a huge crowd? Get to them without too much fear of being caught after you do whatever it is you're planning to do? *Y, por favor, no me diga nada acerca de su estafa,*"[3] *Jaime* added quickly. "*No deseo saber sobre eso.*"[4]

*Carlos* pulled out a twenty-*peso* note and smiled an evil smile. "Can you really help me do this?" he asked the bellman.

---

1. A Trustworthy Secret Agent
2. At Eight O'clock in the Evening
3. "And, please don't tell me about your scheme."
4. "I don't want to know about it."

*Jaime* refused the money with a shake of his hand. Then he answered *Carlos'* question. "*Sí, señor, es posible. Pero es muy complicado, sumamente complicado.*[5] I will have to call in many favors and, as the Gringos might say, 'twist a few arms' here and there. But I can do it if you wish. It will be expensive for me."

"*¿Cuánto, Jaime?*"[6] *Carlos* asked, reaching into his fanny pack for more *pesos*.

Without a pause, *Jaime* answered, "At least *dos mil quinientos pesos, señor.*[7] This is not easy for me to do. But for you, my friend, I can make it happen."

*Carlos* feigned shock.

Then, seeing *Jaime* wasn't going to back off the price, the puma conceded. "Half now, and half when everything's all set."

*Jaime* held out his hand and took the first half of the payment. "*Gracias, señor,*" he said. "I'll be back in two hours. You'll be glad you've invested in *Jaime.*"

\* \* \*

*En el Suite de los Gatos y Cincinnati*[8]

"Do you think we can both play in the game, Luigi?" Luisa asked, hoping to get in a little soccer in the park in front of a big crowd without messing up the chances of a clean capture of *Carlos*.

"Yes, I think so, Luisa, but only one at a time. One of us

---

5. "Yes, sir. It's possible. But very complicated, extremely complicated."
6. "How much, Jaime?"
7. 2,500 pesos
8. In the Cats and Cincinnati's Suite

has to concentrate on *Carlos* every minute. So we'll substitute for one another. How's that?"

"I want to wear *número diez*,"[9] Luisa mentioned casually, trying to see if she could slip one over on her little brother.

"No way, Luisa," Luigi said. "That's the number of the famous *Maradona*,[10] and I'm wearing it for sure."

*Teniente* Chuck, overhearing the kittens' conversation, made a suggestion. "Since you'll be substituting for one another and won't be on the field at the same time, why not both wear *Maradona's número diez?* Perhaps then both of you will score goals, no?"

Luisa smiled at Chuck. "Great idea, just-plain-Chuck, but can we each have a shirt? I don't want to be changing shirts in front of all those people." Nodding toward her brother, she added, "And I sure don't want to wear a shirt that Luigi's been sweating in. Yuck!"

There was a knock on the door. Dusty went to it, but before she opened it, she peeked carefully through the little round peephole to be sure whoever was knocking wasn't *Carlos*, or any other puma, for that matter.

She turned to Chuck, Buzzer and Cincinnati and said, "It's *la Capitán Paloma*."

Luisa replied, *"Pues, entonces abra la puerta,"*[11] and instantly figured she had made two mistakes—telling Dusty what to do, and daring to speak Spanish to her.

Luigi laughed, which didn't help Luisa's standing with Dusty at all.

---

9. number ten
10. *Diego Maradona*, national *fútbol* hero in Argentina
11. "Well, open the door then."

*Capitán Pérez* was smiling when she entered the room. She seemed less worried than Buzzer could remember her being over the last couple of days.

"I have good news and bad news," the captain announced, and went on without pause, "The good news is that *Jaime* is now sure that *Carlos* will slip into our trap. The puma's already paid our secret agent a large sum of money to arrange to get close to Buzzer and Cincinnati, even though *Jaime* hasn't told *Carlos* how he will make that happen yet. He'll pay more when he hears how he's to get there."

"What's the bad news?" Cincinnati wanted to know.

"It's not all that bad, Cincinnati," the captain replied. "It's just that the weather forecast for the day after tomorrow gives a pretty good chance for rain. That, of course, will not stop the game. And it won't keep the huge crowd at home. Here we live for *fútbol*, rain or shine, as you would say. But it might be a little uncomfortable if it's both raining and cool. The weather won't be bad enough to interfere with flying a helicopter, though, Cincinnati and Dusty."

*Capitán Paloma* was almost breathless as she went on. "But I do have more good news for you. The bleachers will be set up tomorrow morning, and the field will be lined off. Goals will be set up at each end of the field. And the *equipo de gatitos de Brasil*[12] is scheduled to arrive in the afternoon." Now turning to Chuck, she asked, "How are we coming with pulling together the Argentinean team, *teniente?*"

"We're ready, *capitán*," Chuck answered. "*Tenemos catorce*

---

12. team of kittens from Brazil

*jugadores de Argentina y* Luigi y Luisa—*un total de diez y seis.*[13] And the suspense is building. I heard a few minutes ago that ticket sales are booming. The producers are projecting a crowd of more than *cincuenta mil personas.*"[14]

"¡Holy *frijoles!*" said Luigi. "That's a lot of people."

"Yes, Luigi, it is," Buzzer said. Turning to the captain and Chuck, he asked, "What are we missing at this point?"

"Right now," Chuck said, "I think it's important that we all get some sleep.

We can go over all the details in the morning, but for now, everything seems to be going just as Luigi and Luisa planned."

Chuck smiled at the twins and added, *"Muy buen trabajo, gemelos."*[15]

Luigi stood up and saluted Chuck. Luisa, too, was very proud, though she still thought Luigi had somehow cheated when they drew straws to see who would get to present the plan.

✶ ✶ ✶

*En el Meteoro en el Río de La Plata*

*Ramos* had decided that since the authorities already had a record of him being in Argentina he might as well go left into the old port at *Puerto Madero* in *Buenos Aires.*

As he eased the *Meteoro* into a slip between the older Navy ship *Sarmiento* and the new *Libertad*, he marveled at

---

13. "We have fourteen players from Argentina, and Luigi and Luisa—sixteen
   total."
14. 50,000 people
15. "Very good work, twins."

the changes in *Puerto Madero*. Used to be, he thought, these beautiful buildings were nothing more than abandoned warehouses, dirty and boarded up, some crumbling into piles of rubble. Now I see they've been rebuilt and turned into chic shops, fine restaurants and dealers of expensive automobiles. Since I have money for once in my life, I believe I'll treat myself to a good meal and a bottle of fine wine at one of these restaurants. Then I'll come back to my boat and watch the late news, to see if that fugitive puma *Carlos* has been captured yet.

As *Ramos* finished tying up the *Meteoro* and started to walk toward one of the waterside restaurants, he saw two port policemen coming toward him. Instinctively, he flinched and started looking for a place to hide, or at least to be as invisible as possible.

"*Buenos noches, señor*," one of the port policemen said to Ramos as they passed on the wide walkway next to the boat slips.

*Ramos* responded quietly, "*Buenos noches*," and slipped quickly into the shadow of a big tropical tree. I have to stop acting as if I've done something wrong, *Ramos* thought. I'm going to make trouble for myself by seeming to be guilty. And guilty of what? I've done nothing wrong. Of course I haven't. Nobody ever needs to know about the money *Carlos* paid me, do they? And now I'll spend a small amount of it on *un bistec grande y una botella de buen vino*.[16] Maybe I'll go to the big *fútbol* match in two days.

Unless *Carlos* is caught first, that is.

---

16. a big steak and a bottle of fine wine

# * LOS GATOS OF THE CIA: TANGO WITH A PUMA *

## * * *

*En el Bar Maximiliano en el Vestíbulo del Hotel*

Knowing *Carlos* to be, at times, a "mean motor scooter," *Jaime* had decided to call the puma's room and ask to meet with him in the lobby bar, a more public place. It was 10:00 in the evening as he walked from behind the bar to look for the puma. At that hour, the bar was still fairly quiet. The revelers would show up in another hour or two.

*Jaime* found the puma sitting in a remote corner, as far from both the bar and the piano as possible. Having changed from his bellman's uniform into slacks and a sport shirt, *Jaime* sat down at a small round table across from *Carlos*. They would seem to be just *los dos empresarios*[17] having an evening drink and an innocent conversation.

"Have you made the arrangements yet?" *Carlos* asked immediately. "How are you going to get me right in front of the cat and the pig?"

"Everything's arranged, *señor*," *Jaime* said. "But first I have to ask you a few questions."

"*¿Qué?*"[18] *Carlos* asked.

"I have to be sure you know all the rules of *el juego de fútbol*.[19] Do you?"

"But of course. As a child and young puma, *fútbol* was my life. Why do you ask this question? What does it have to do with the cat and the pig?"

"Do you not remember the news I asked you to watch

---

17. two businessmen
18. "What?"
19. the game of soccer

only three hours ago?" *Jaime* answered. "The big *fútbol* match between the small cats of *Brasil y Argentina pasado mañana?*"[20]

"*Sí, yo recuerdo bien.*[21] But what does that have to do with me, the cat and the pig, *Jaime*? You're talking in riddles."

"Do you not think the cat and the pig—and the other three cats, too—will be there? Maybe the little cats will even be playing in the match, no?"

*Carlos* still was confused. "I'm still not following you, *Jaime*. So the cat and the pig will be there, but how does that get me in front of them?"

"How would you like to be the official *árbitro*[22] of that match? You would be in control of the game and be able to move up and down the field and along the sidelines.

You could even have an associate help you spot your prey. And then, at halftime or after the match, 'wham,' you lower the boom on them, or whatever it is you plan to do. How's that?"

"You can do this for me, *Jaime*?" *Carlos* seemed unbelieving.

"It's a done deal, *señor*. That is, if you say 'yes' and pay me another 1,250 *pesos*. What do you say?" *Jaime* smiled at the big puma like the cat who ate the canary.

"I say '*Sí, sí,*' *Jaime*. But it must be understood that I'm a traveling salesman, a salesman of rocking horses for the children, *¿Verdad?*" *Carlos* insisted. "Can you be sure of that?"

---

20. the day after tomorrow
21. Yes, I remember well.
22. referee

*Jaime* smiled and said, "Are you not simply a traveling salesman of children's rocking horses, *señor*? That's what I've told my associates, and—if it's not true—I don't want to know. And no one else will ever know."

As he slipped the equivalent of more than 350 U.S. dollars under the table and into *Jaime*'s hand, *Carlos* chuckled wickedly and said to the bellman, "*Sin duda, yo soy un vendedor de caballitos para los niños, Jaime.*[23] Who else could I possibly be?"

*Do you think Carlos will be able to fool the big crowd into believing he's really a traveling salesman who has taken time off to referee the big Copa de Caperucita Roja? What do you think the puma wants to do to Buzzer and Cincinnati? Will he try to hurt Luigi or Luisa? Or maybe cheat their team out of a goal if one of them should score? Will it rain? If it does, can Cincinnati and Dusty see well enough from the helicopter?*

---

23. Without doubt, I am a salesman of children's rocking horses, *Jaime*.

# Aprendamos a Hablar en Español
by Dusty Louise

*Tal vez, hay muchos miembros en su familia. ¿Cómo se les llama?* [24]

| In English | In Spanish | Say It Like This |
| --- | --- | --- |
| Parents | *Los padres* | lohs PAH-drehs |
| Mother | *Madre, Mami* | MAH-dreh, MAH-mee |
| Father | *Padre, Papi* | PAH-dreh, PAH-pee |
| Son | *Hijo* | EE-hoh |
| Daughter | *Hija* | EE-hah |
| Brother | *Hermano* | air-MAH-noh |
| Sister | *Hermana* | air-MAH-nah |
| Grandmother | *Abuela* | ah-BWAY-lah |
| Grandfather | *Abuelo* | Ah-BWAY-loh |
| Grandson | *Nieto* | nee-AY-toh |
| Granddaughter | *Nieta* | Nee-AY-tah |
| Uncle | *Tío* | TEE-oh |
| Aunt | *Tía* | TEE-ah |
| Niece | *Sobrina* | soh-BREE-nah |
| Nephew | *Sobrino* | soh-BREE-noh |
| Male cousin | *Primo* | PREE-moh |
| Female cousin | *Prima* | PREE-mah |

---

24. Maybe there are many members in your family. How do you say their names?

# * Chapter 17 *
# Zona Cero[1]

*Antes de La Copa de Caperucita Roja*[2]

Chuck gathered the sixteen Argentinean kindergarten kittens, in their light blue and white shirts with yellow numbers, into a tight circle on the sideline of the big soccer field. *Ayer, La Presidente de Argentina*[3] had named the *teniente* coach of his country's team. Chuck spoke to them over the noise of the huge crowd that was quickly filling the bleachers.

"*Gatitos, escúchenme, por favor,*"[4] Chuck began as *diez y seis*[5] pairs of little eyes locked on him and waited for words of wisdom and encouragement. Chuck continued, "This is, of course, a big and important *fútbol* match. You are here in these beautiful shirts because you are the best of the best players in our country. Our friends from Brazil are also very

---

1. Ground Zero
2. Before the Little Red Riding Hood Cup
3. Yesterday, the president of Argentina
4. Kittens, listen to me, please.
5. Sixteen

good. So stick to your game. Play hard. Play smart. Do what you know how to do, and everything will be just fine. Win or lose, it's an honor for all of us to be here today." He concluded by clapping his hands together three times and adding, "Always be good sports."

Luisa leaned over and spoke into Luigi's ear. "Can we always be good sports if we have to go into 'Plan B,' Luigi?"

"Shhh," Luigi cautioned. "Nobody but you and I knows anything about 'Plan B.' Maybe we won't have to use it at all, and then there'll be no problem. But if my guess is right, we'll have to use it. These soccer fans in South America get pretty worked up, you know. Worse than the Brits, at times. And if we do use it, it'll help us capture *Carlos*. That's the only way we can, Luisa, if it will make capturing that puma easier. Or even possible."

Luisa nodded. "Look, Luigi, there's the *árbitro*[6] walking onto the center of the field. I smell puma. I smell *Carlos*."

Luigi sniffed the air and nodded, and then he changed the subject, as usual. "You start the game, Luisa, at right wing. I'll substitute for you after about *ocho o diez minutos. Buena suerte, hermanita.*"[7]

* * *

*Sobre el Tejado del Hospital en el Centro de Buenos Aires*[8]

Cincinnati adjusted the right cockpit seat in the shiny blue-and-white Bell Jet Ranger. As he slipped into the safety harness, he turned to Dusty Louise in the left seat beside

---

6. referee
7. eight or ten minutes. Good luck, little sister.
8. On the Hospital Roof in Downtown *Buenos Aires*

him. *"Los helicópteros son diferentes a los aviones,*[9] Dusty. You fly them much differently. I'll teach you sometime, but today I need you to handle the binoculars and the radio. You keep *Carlos* in sight and stay in radio contact with Buzzer Louis and *Capitán Paloma* on the sidelines behind the *teniente*. Go ahead and pull on your headset. Let's get this bird in the air."

A light rain began to fall as Cincinnati cranked up the Jet Ranger, but the cloud ceiling was still above 3,000 feet. Dusty Louise and Cincinnati would have no trouble keeping an eye the big puma in the black-and-white striped shirt.

*El árbitro oficial.*

✳ ✳ ✳

*En las Tribunas del Campo de Fútbol*[10]

*Jaime,* after delivering *Carlos el árbitro* to his official pregame position, joined Buzzer Louis and *Capitán Paloma* on the first row of the bleachers—right behind *el equipo de gatitos de Argentina.*[11] *Jaime's* K-9 partner, *Basko,* joined them.

*Jaime* sat slumped over, a *sombrero grande*[12] pulled down low on his forehead to hide his eyes and entire face, for that matter, from being seen by *Carlos* from the field.

The captain turned toward Buzzer. "So far, so good," she said.

Buzzer couldn't decide if she was commenting on the

---

9. Helicopters are different from airplanes
10. In the grandstands of the Soccer Field
11. The team of kittens from Argentina
12. big hat

progress of the plan or just expressing some wishful thinking that the plan devised by Luigi and Luisa would work —
work like they all imagined and believed it should.

"*Sí, Capitán,*" Buzzer answered, "with a big 'thank you'
to *Jaime* here for single-handedly delivering *Carlos* to us. My
big concern all along has been the size of this crowd. I
didn't say anything because I didn't want to take away from
the cleverness the twins showed in plotting all this. But,
wherever there are 50,000 partisan and almost rabid soccer
fans, there's always the danger of some kind of riot. That
could complicate the capture." Buzzer exhaled. "So cross
your fingers this crowd behaves itself." The loudspeaker system blared as the players from each team were introduced.
As Luisa ran onto the field after being announced as 'Luisa
Manicotti Giaccomazza *de Estados Unidos,*' a huge roar went
up because of her number ten shirt—*Diego Maradona*'s number. Another *número diez* followed with 'Luigi Panettone
Giaccomazza *de Estados Unidos,*' and the crowd went wild,
stomping and yelling at the top of their lungs.

*Carlos* set the ball in the center of the field and told the
*Brasileño* team they, as visitors, had the option to kick off or
receive.

They chose to kick, and the game was on.

For the first five or six minutes, the two teams parried
back and forth, sizing up one another's skills as attackers
and defenders. Then, six and a half minutes into the first
half, Luisa, taking a pass from a halfback from *Tigre,*[13] broke

---

13. A suburb north of *Buenos Aires*

away from the fullback who was crowding her, feinted past the goalie and softly rolled the *fútbol* into the net.

*Argentina*—1. *Brasil*—0. The crowd went crazy.

As Luisa came off the field, passing her little brother who would take her place, Luigi gave her a high-four and shouted over the din of the crowd, "You're the best, *hermanita*. I'm proud of you!"

Throughout the rest of the first half, the rain continued to fall softly. Cincinnati and Dusty hovered in the Jet Ranger, posing as a television crew, at about 600 feet—high enough to avoid being a noisy distraction, but low enough to keep a close eye on the big puma.

Luigi and Luisa alternately played and sat out–with the one not playing keeping both eyes glued on *Carlos*.

As the first half ended, with Argentina still leading 1-0 on Luisa's breakaway goal, Dusty called Buzzer on the radio. "What's the next move, Buzzer?" she asked. "Have you set a definite time to spring the puma trap?"

Buzz answered her so that *Basko*, a big black and brown Rottweiler, *Jaime y la capitán* could also hear. "Just as the game ends, Dusty, in another forty-five minutes or so. The old Peugeot's ready, if there's not too much confusion. And you can see that a whole block of *Avenida Sarmiento* has been blocked off with barricades and ropes so you and Cincinnati can set down the helicopter if we need to use it to get *Carlos* out of here.

"How's your fuel?" Buzz added.

"Plenty of go-juice," Cincinnati answered. "Fuel's no problem. Please tell the *capitán* that this new Jet Ranger is a fine aircraft. It handles well in the rain, for sure."

* * *

*Del Segundo Tiempo*[14]

As the second half began, with Argentina kicking off, a striker from *Brasil* leaped up, headed the ball downfield, and outraced the defenders to drive straight past the Argentine goalie and into the net.

Just like that, the score was 1-1.

For the next forty minutes or so, nobody scored. Each team drove the ball down the field, but failed to score. The game was back-and-forth, and the teams were evenly matched. Oh, there was lots of action, but the defenders were up to the challenge.

With about four minutes left in the match, Luisa—on a give-and-go with the same halfback from *Tigre*—broke away from an off-balance defender, and, this time, smashed the ball straight into the net for what seemed would be a lead for Argentina.

*Carlos*, however, blew his whistle, waved both front paws over his head and claimed that Luisa had been offside.

Goal denied.

The partisan Argentine crowd shouted obscenities at *Carlos*, who had, in fact, been out of position to actually see when Luisa received the pass. And he had made a bad call.

Luisa came off the field dejected as the crowd alternately shouted, "*¡Maradona!*" and "*¡Muerte al árbitro!*"[15]

Luigi went into the game for a discouraged Luisa, who sat down with her head hung low, so low she almost forgot

---

14. The Second Half
15. "Death to the referee!"

to keep an eagle eye on *Carlos*. She whispered a secret into *Jaime*'s ear: what he and *Basko* would need to do if Luigi called for "Plan B."

*Jaime* nodded and turned to Buzzer and *Capitán Paloma*. "These twins are very clever. They always have a back-up plan. Don't worry, Buzzer and *capitán*. We'll have that puma in custody within five minutes. Luisa and Luigi guarantee it."

As the match resumed, Luigi and the halfback from *Tigre* immediately pulled the same give-and-go trick, and this time Luigi faked the goalie straight to the ground and headed the ball into the net for another apparent goal.

But *Carlos* remained consistent, ruling that Luigi, this time, had been offside.

No goal allowed.

This was his second questionable call in less than a minute, and the crowd suddenly went berserk. Cups and cushions rained down from the bleachers onto the field. Spectators began to spill out of the stands and stalk along the sidelines.

Luigi ran over to where Luisa and the *teniente* were standing in disbelief and shouted as loudly as he could, "Plan B. Execute Plan B!"

Luisa grabbed the portable communications radio from Buzzer and keyed the microphone. "Dusty, Cincinnati! Bring the chopper over the field in one minute, as soon as you see the crowd rush the field. Get ready to drop the harnesses."

Speechless, Buzzer stared at her. He thought, What are these two up to now? But he pretended all was okay and that he was in on the action, so as not to worry *Capitán*

*Paloma* and have her maybe take matters into her own hands and start barking orders.

It was time to trust Luigi and Luisa. They'd been right so far, hadn't they?

With the crowd agitated and restless, though still semi-orderly, *Carlos* resumed the game.

Immediately Luigi ran to the center of the field, leapt in the air past the referee, and swiped *Carlos* across the top of the head with open claws, knocking off the big puma's black referee's hat.

Plan B was in play.

A stunned *Carlos* first reacted by picking up his cap and putting it back on his head. Then he reached into his shirt pocket and pulled out *una tarjeta roja.*[16] He would toss that number ten out of this game, whichever of the number tens it happened to be.

Luigi, expecting the red card, stopped and stuck out his tongue at *Carlos.* He gave the puma a raspberry almost loud enough to be heard over the din of the crowd, a crowd that had enjoyed, even approved of, Luigi's little attack.

*Carlos,* now furious, took off after Luigi to serve him with the red card.

Luigi, hoping to create total pandemonium, ran on and off the field, into and out of the milling crowd. All the while he was shouting, *"¡Muerte al árbitro. Muerte al árbitro!"*

Soon the crowd took up the chant again. Then fans began to move onto the field . . . to close a tight circle around *el gatito Norteamericano y el árbitro malo.*[17]

---

16. a red card
17. North American kitten and the bad referee

Luigi ran.

*Carlos*, losing all sense of reality, chased him.

The circle being tightened by the unhappy crowd got smaller and smaller, until only Luigi and the puma were inside it.

Cincinnati and Dusty brought the helicopter in low—to no higher than sixty feet. Dusty lowered a cable attached to two body harnesses used for rescues.

Suddenly *Carlos* came out of his confused state. He knew he was in trouble.

Big time.

His eyes opened wide. He looked up, then his glance darted to all sides, eyes growing larger still. What was going on here?

Frantic, *Carlos* looked for a crack in the inner wall of the circle of spectators slowly closing in on him and the taunting little Number Ten cat.

But he saw only *Basko y Jaime*, breaking through the wall and coming to his rescue.

*Jaime* and *Basko* rushed up to *Carlos* as the angry crowd closed in.

"I'm here to save you, *Señor Vendedor*," *Jaime* shouted into the puma's left ear, taking him firmly by the shoulder and grabbing the rescue harness dangling from the helicopter with his free hand.

"Here, snap this around your chest. I'll go with you. Hold onto me!" *Jaime* yelled to *Carlos*.

By now, the puma was ready to be saved.

As *Carlos* snapped the harness and grabbed onto *Jaime*,

Luisa keyed the radio and said to Cincinnati and Dusty, "Take it up! Pull it up! Now!"

With a jerk, *Carlos el puma, Basko el perro, y Jaime, el agente secreto botones*[18] were lifted into the air. Dusty was reeling in the rescue cable at top speed as Cincinnati banked, turned the helicopter toward *PFA* headquarters downtown, and gained altitude.

Cincinnati's voice came over the radio loud and clear. "One puma in tow. One secret agent holding a .45-caliber Glock Police Special against the side of his head. One fierce looking K-9 latched onto the puma's leg. One somewhat impatient, but very pretty, little gray tabby cat wrapping bungee cords around and around the puma. One flying, dancing pig headed for the *PFA* helipad. Grab that old Peugeot, Buzzer, and we'll meet you guys there." Cincinnati concluded as the blue and white Jet Ranger disappeared over the trees, headed south.

*Who do you think will really be the winner of the soccer match, since the score was tied and the game never actually ended? Will Cincinnati, Dusty,* Basko *and* Jaime *be able to get* Carlos *into jail without getting hurt, or having him escape? What about Luigi and Luisa? Do you think they'll feel cheated that their goals didn't count? And will Buzzer, the captain and the lieutenant be able to get through that angry crowd and get to PFA headquarters anytime soon? Maybe in the old Peugeot?*

---

18. *Carlos* the puma, *Basko* the dog, and *Jaime*, the secret agent bellman

# Aprendamos a Hablar en Español
by Dusty Louise

*Hay muchos tipos de animales en América del Sur. ¿Cómo se les llama por sus nombres?* [19]

| In English | In Spanish | Say It Like This |
| --- | --- | --- |
| Cat | Gato | GAH=toh |
| Kitten | Gatito | gah-TEE-toh |
| Dog | Perro | PAIR-roh |
| Bird | Pájaro | PAH-hah-roh |
| Donkey | Burro | BOO-roh |
| Pig | Cerdo | SAIR-doh |
| Parrot | Loro | LOH-roh |
| Bear | Oso | OH-soh |
| Eagle | Aguila | ah-GWEE-lah |
| Tiger | Tigre | TEE-greh |
| Turtle | Tortuga | tohr-TOO-gah |
| Wolf | Lobo | LOH-boh |
| Snake | Culebra | coo-LAY-brah |
| Fox | Zorro | ZOHR-roh |
| Horse | Caballo | cah-BY-zhoh |
| Cow | Vaca | VAH-cah |
| Sheep | Oveja | oh-VAY-hah |
| Goat | Cabra | CAH-brah |
| Skunk | Zorillo | zoh-REE-zhoh |
| Armadillo | Armadillo | ahr-mah-DEE-zhoh |
| Fish | Pescado | pehs-CAH-doh |
| Cougar | Puma | POO-mah |

*armadillo?*  *¡armadillo!*

19. There are many kinds of animals in South America. How do you say their names?

# * Epilogue *
# Exposición del Tango[1]

*La Oficina de PFA Después del Juego*[2]

"You tricked me. You lied to me!" *Carlos* shrieked.

The big cat sat cuffed to a chair that was bolted to the floor, in a small room across the hallway from the sound-proof interrogation room. He was furious. And he was more than a little embarrassed to have fallen for such a scam.

*Jaime* stood just inside the small room's doorway. The door was halfway open.

"No, *Señor Vendedor*," *Jaime* answered calmly. "I wouldn't do that to someone of honor such as yourself. Because I, too, am a person of honor."

"Baloney!" *Carlos* screamed.

"Be calm, *Carlos*," *Jaime* said, adding, "Yes, I do know who you really are. But I have done exactly everything I promised you. Did I not arrange for you to be the *árbitro* for the biggest *fútbol* match of the year, just as I said I would

---

1. Tango Show
2. The *PFA* Office after the Game

do? Did I not deliver you safely to the *campo* where the match was to be played? Did I not even rescue and bring you to safety from an angry mob shouting '*¡Muerte al árbitro!*?'"

Seething, *Carlos* interrupted him. "*Sí, Jaime*, but what about the cat and the pig? Huh? What about them? You promised to put me in front of them today, but that did not happen."

"Patience, *señor*," *Jaime* said softly as Cincinnati and Buzzer Louis walked into the room and stood in front of the big puma. "Here they are, as promised," *Jaime* smiled.

\* \* \*

*En el Cuarto de Interrogación*

Luigi, Luisa and Dusty sat quietly around the table where the plans had been hatched and the details worked out for the successful capture of *Carlos*. The twins were tired from a long soccer match, but they were excited that both their stupendous plan and their secret Plan B had worked . .. to perfection.

Dusty was just plain tired. But she had to admit she was also very proud of *los gemelos*. Maybe they were truly beginning to grow up. She thought, I'll miss them as babies, but I don't think they'll ever outgrow being pranksters. We can all enjoy their pranks for a long time to come.

The silence broke as Chuck walked in with four big bowls of *helado dulce de leche* on a tray. "This is my favorite flavor, *amigos*, he said. It's *dulce de leche*."

Dusty looked confused. "How would you translate that to English, Chuck?" she asked. "Sweet milk?"

"Not really," Chuck said, smiling at Dusty. "I think it just does not translate. Any way you try to say it in English doesn't come out right. Why not just stick with '*dulce de leche?*'"

Luigi, in particular, was ready to dig in, but both he and Luisa still had unanswered questions for Chuck.

"Can we talk while we eat some of it?" Luisa asked. "We have a lot of important loose ends to tie together here, Chuck. At least they're important to us."

Chuck set a big bowl and spoon in front of each of the four. "Sure, eat and ask. What would you like to know, Luisa and Luigi?"

"To begin with," Luigi said, "who won the game? Luisa and I both scored goals that *Carlos el árbitro* cheated us out of. He must be blind."

"Under the rules of FIFA, Luigi, the international *fútbol* authority, the game was not finished. So FIFA at first said there could be no winner. However, both coaches and the representatives of both countries agreed, in the interest of better relations between *Brasil y Argentina*, the first Little Red Riding Hood Cup should go in the record book as a tie, one to one."

"But we really scored three goals," Luisa protested. "I scored two myself!"

"Yes, almost everyone, even the *gatitos de Brasil*, agreed that both your goals looked fair to them. So they have graciously offered that for the coming year—until the next

*Copa de Caperucita Roja*—the beautiful trophy should remain here in *Buenos Aires* for all to see," Chuck said.

Luigi, swallowing a big chunk of *dulce de leche*, said, "That's very nice of them, I guess, but Luisa and I are going home tomorrow. We won't get to see it whenever we want—maybe never again. Somehow that doesn't seem quite right to me." Adding in his own patented form of jump-speak, he said, "Say, this *helado* is really good, just-plain-Chuck."

Luisa still looked a little disappointed, although it was clear from how quickly she was putting down the ice cream that she agreed with Luigi's last comment.

"But I do have news that may make the two of you feel better," Chuck said.

"What's that, just-plain-Chuck?" Luisa asked.

"The players on both teams have voted Luisa Manicotti Giaccomazza and Luigi Panettone Giaccomazza the 'Most Valuable Players' of the first *Copa de Caperucita Roja.* Congratulations!" Chuck applauded softly, and Dusty Louise joined in.

The twins beamed and high-foured one another.

Chuck let them share their glory for a moment and then said, "Now I have a question for the two of you."

"What's that, just-plain-Chuck?" Luigi asked, still celebrating with his twin sister.

"When are you going to need the two *gaucho* disguises you asked for?" Chuck asked.

Luisa winked at Luigi. Luigi winked back at her. The two of them burst into laughter.

"Now, Chuck!" Luigi answered as Luisa nodded her

head a vigorous 'yes.' "Get them and have Buzzer and Cincinnati put them on right away," Luigi said.

Chuck looked obviously confused, but Dusty got the joke. She said to him, "It's another one of their pranks, just-plain-Chuck. They want to see Buzzer and Cincinnati dressed up and looking funny."

She smiled and shook her head side to side—as if giving in to the never-ending pranks that come when you live with these tiny twins.

The twins shrugged in unison and gave her their best Alfred E. Neuman[3] faces, as if to say, "Who? Us? Would we do that?"

Chuck laughed and said, "Then I need to take you all back to the *Hotel Sheraton Libertador*. *Capitán Paloma* has tickets for all of us to go to *una exposición de tango* later this evening. Let me find Cincinnati and just-plain-Buzzer and get them into their costumes so we can go back to the hotel."

* * *

*En la Calle Enfrente de las Oficinas de PFA*[4]

News of *Carlos'* capture had spread like wildfire before a strong wind. A large crowd gathered across the street from *PFA* headquarters, as if expecting to see or hear something dramatic.

*Capitán Ramos* stood in the front ranks right up against

---

3. Alfred E. Neuman is a funny-looking little cartoon boy with big ears, freckles, buck teeth and a blank expression who graced the covers of MAD Magazine for fifty years.
4. On the Street in Front of PFA Headquarters

the curb, a small *valija*[5] sitting on the sidewalk next to him. He was trying to make yet another decision in his confusion to protect himself from further questioning, yet still keep the money *Carlos* had paid him—and maybe get even more. His thoughts flashed back and forth like a tennis ball in a fast match.

*Carlos* has more money. A lot of it, he thought. I had nothing to do with his capture, and he knows that, I think. I could leave and just keep the money I have right now. Or, maybe I could be really, really rich.

Just then he saw a sight that distracted him from his debate with himself: four cats and a pig came out with a tall man in a pinstriped suit. They all climbed into an unmarked dark blue Fiat cruiser and drove away. But one of the cats—the biggest one—and the pig were dressed as *gauchos*, cowboys. And the pig was almost dancing.

*¡Qué curioso!*[6] *Ramos* said to himself, idly.

Shaking his head in wonder, he went back to watching the front doors across the street. He watched as if he were waiting for someone to come out, or something to happen.

✳ ✳ ✳

*En la Gran Exposición del Tango*[7]

After a fine dinner, a talented group of five musicians and eight dancers were putting on a spectacular show featuring the dance that originated in *Buenos Aires*—the tango.

Luigi and Luisa had taken a couple of lessons from the

---

5. suitcase
6. How curious!
7. At the Big Tango Show

dancers before the show. Now, to the delight of the crowd and the performers, they were doing their own Hill Country version of a fast tango on the edge of the big stage.

Luisa thought the dancers were just gorgeous . . . and very athletic.

Luigi liked the percussionist with a big kettle drum and two *bolos* with metal balls on their ends the best.

Dusty was thinking, I'm as pretty as any of these dancers. And I can fly an airplane. I'll bet none of them can do that.

As the show came to an end, all the performers stood in the stage lights and sang '*No Llores por Mí, Argentina*'— 'Don't Cry for Me, Argentina'—from the musical *Evita*, each waving a full-sized *bandera de Argentina*.[8]

At the stroke of *medianoche*,[9] just as the performers finished and were taking bows to the applause of the audience, the lights flickered and, immediately, a window-rattling explosion shook the building.

Chuck grabbed his cell phone and raced to a corner of the second floor dining room near the elevator, speed-dialing as he went. He listened for only a few seconds and then returned.

"*Capitán*," he said to the captain so all at the table could hear, "Our headquarters has just been bombed. *Carlos* the puma has escaped. He was seen running out the door with a man who had come in earlier claiming to be his lawyer, but the man smelled of fish. *Hernando* said he didn't believe he was a lawyer at all. After the explosion, they jumped into

8. Argentinean flag
9. midnight

a long black Mercedes limousine. A guard at the front doors heard the other man tell the driver, *'Puerto Madero.'*"

Buzzer turned to Cincinnati and said, "Well, I guess I'd better call Dr. Buford Lewis and Bogart-BOGART back at home. It's not late there now. But what do you think I ought to tell them, Cincinnati?"

The dancing pig looked tired. He sighed, "Tell them we'll be back in the Hill Country tomorrow night. But we may not be staying too long."

*El Fin*[10]

---

10. The End

# ¡Un Millión de Gracias![1]

To produce a book like *Tango with a Puma* takes months of research, about 15,000 miles of travel, making a couple of Spanish-English dictionaries and a big book of 1,000 conjugated Spanish verbs dog-eared, followed by a lot of writing, rewriting, correcting, changing and perspiration.

And that's just on the part of the author.

Many others have participated in the process.

At Eakin Press, publisher now of seven of my books, thanks to Tom Messer and Kris Gholson for their advice, ever-ready response and just doing what they do so well. Thanks also to my editor, Janis Williams, who did an extraordinarily thorough job and taught me some of the finer points of style and context. She left my manuscript much better than she found it. To Pat Molenaar, book designer, and Kim Williams, cover designer, for dressing up the finished product fit to go to a big tango show.

Jason Eckhardt has now illustrated five of my seven books. He's an incredible talent, as anyone can see, bringing my characters—both animal and human—to life and making the way they look true to their individual personalities.

In *Buenos Aires, el botones del Hotel Sheraton Libertador* was an incredibly helpful and knowledgeable young man, *Daniel Roca*. *Gracias, amigo*. Your first edition copy is on the way to you.

---

1. A Million Thanks

Thanks also to *Corporal Horacio Conde* of the *PFA* for patiently and quickly outlining the various divisions of the *Policía Federal de Argentina*. I am also grateful to a dozen taxi drivers in BA for politely answering stupid Gringo questions, and to the people of that beautiful city for their civility and graciousness.

Special thanks and extra credit also goes to Gadylu Espinosa, a superb translator who made my sometimes-botched *Español* actually say what it was supposed to say. A native of Tampico, México, Gady added the special knowledge not only of her native tongue, but also of the variations to that language as spoken in Argentina.

Extra special thanks go to my brother, retired United Airlines Captain Jim Arnold, who served not only as a clever resource for information about *Buenos Aires* (where he had spent many a layover during his flying days), but also as a pretty good travel agent in arranging for a trip of multiple flights, as well as serving as my backup legs on-site when a callus on the bottom of one of my feet reared its ugly self at the most inopportune of times. Jim is responsible for discovering *la estatua de Caperucita Roja*. Being a little weird himself (it runs in the genes), he thought maybe it was offbeat enough to be included in the book. Good call.

Finally, my undying gratitude to a dedicated group of manuscript readers who suffered through the second draft a chapter at a time and made remarkably good observations about how to improve it. These people have no real idea how valuable their participation has been. Shhh, don't tell them or they may want more than a signed and personalized first edition as their reward.

*Dallas, Texas*
Edward Stone, Chairman Emeritus, The Dallas Marketing Group
Peter Sawyer, The Other Grandfather to the Amazing Liam
Elena Turner, Bilingual Advertising Executive
Marilyn Pippin, Public Relations Agency President, Cat Lover
Gadylu Espinosa, Translator

*Bandera, Texas*
   Suzy Groff, ELA Teacher, Bandera Middle School
   Krista Errington, ELA Teacher, Bandera Middle School
   Shay McMullan, Sixth Grade Student, sailor, animal lover, sister
   Kyle Wilson, Sixth Grade Student
   Ricardo Espinosa, Seventh Grade Student
   Ethan Greven, A shrewd individual, quarterback of the seventh grade football team, and A+ student
   Sara Herrera, Eighth Grade Student
   Brittany Palacios, Eighth Grade Student

*Houston, Texas*
   Julie B. Fix, APR, Associate Professor, University of Houston
   Mary Turrin, Substitute Teacher
   Noah Turrin, Fourth Grade Student

*Phoenix, Arizona*
   Steve Dodd, Realtor

*Rockport, Texas*
   Bert Haney, Unknown Children's Book Author, Retired TV News Director

*Portland, Oregon*
   Joe James, Retired Advertising Executive and author of ten books (and "Really Nice Guy")

*San Antonio, Texas*
   Ken Squier, Retired Movie Exhibitor Executive

*New Bedford, Massachusetts*
   Jason Eckhardt, Illustrator

*Seattle, Washington*
   Barbara Ivancich, Ad Agency Accounting Executive
   Marion Woodfield, Ad Agency Accounting Executive

*Irvine, California*
 Margery Arnold, Ph.D., Child Psychologist
 Mariel Clark, Third Grade Student
 Julianne Clark, Kindergarten Student

*Fort Worth, Texas*
 MacKenzie Errington, Fourth Grade Student

*St. Petersburg, Florida*
 Jim Arnold, Retired Airline Captain
 Barbara Arnold, Sailor, Cat Lover and Grandmother

*Cincinnati, Ohio*
 Deborah Arnold, Teacher and Manuscript Stasher

*San Diego, California*
 Cynthia Voliva, Reformed Journalist and TV News Producer

As always, any mistakes you may find in the book are mine, and mine alone. And, yes, I do know there's no fountain in front of the downtown Sheraton in *Buenos Aires*. But there should be.

—GEORGE ARNOLD
2010

# Glossary and Pronunciation Guide

Following are several hundred everyday Spanish words and phrases, alphabetized by their English translations and including a guide to properly pronouncing them.

| In English | In Spanish | Say It Like This |
|---|---|---|
| **A** | | |
| Airport | *Aeropuerto* | ah-air-oh-PWAIR-toh |
| Airplane | *Avión* | ah-vee-OHN |
| Ankle | *Tobillo* | Toh-BEE-zho |
| April | *Abril* | ah-BREEL |
| Armadillo | *Armadillo* | ahr-mah-DEE-zhoh |
| Arms | *Brazos* | BRAH-szohs |
| August | *Agosto* | ah-GOHS-toh |
| Aunt | *Tía* | TEE-ah |
| Auto racing | *Carreras de coches* | cah-REHR-ahs day COH-chezs |
| | | |
| **B** | | |
| Backpack | *Mochilla* | moh-CHEE-zhzh |
| Bacon | *Tocino* | toh-SEE-noh |
| Baseball | *Béisbol* | BEHS-bohl |
| Basketball | *Baloncesto* | bahl-ohn-SESS-toh |

| | | |
|---|---|---|
| Banana | *Banana* | bah-NAH-nah |
| Bathroom | *Cuarto de baño* | KWAHR-toh day BAH-nyoh |
| Beans | *Frijoles* | free-HOH-lehs |
| Bear | *Oso* | OH-soh |
| Beef | *Bíf, Bife* | BEEF , BEE-feh |
| Bellman | *Botones* | boh-TOH-nehs |
| Belt | *Cinturón* | seen-too-ROHN |
| Bicycle | *Bicicleta* | bee-see-CLAY-tah |
| Bird | *Pájaro* | PAH-hah-roh |
| Black | *Negro* | NAY-groh |
| Blouse | *Blusa* | BLOO-sah |
| Blue | *Azul* | ah-SZOOL |
| Boat | *Bote* | BOH-teh |
| Boots | *Botas* | BOH-tahsz |
| Bowl | *Tazón* | tah-SZOHN |
| Bread | *Pan* | PAHN |
| Breakfast | *Desayuno* | day-seh-OO-noh |
| Brother | *Hermano* | air-MAH-noh |
| Brown | *Marrón, Café* | mah-ROHN, cah-FAY |
| Bus | *Autobús* | ah-oo-toh-BOOSE |
| Butter | *Mantequilla* | mahn-teh-KEE-zhah |

## C

| | | |
|---|---|---|
| Candy | *Bombón, dulce* | bohm-BOHN, DOOL-seh |
| Caramel | *Caramelo* | cahr-ah-MEH-loh |
| Cap | *Gorra* | goh-RAH |
| Captain | *Capitán* | cah-pee-TAHN |
| Car | *Auto* | ah-OO-toh |
| Cat | *Gato* | GAH-toh |
| Catnip | *Nébeda* | NAY-beh-dah |
| Chair | *Silla* | SEE-zhah |

| | | |
|---|---|---|
| Check in (to a hotel) | *Registrarse* | ray-jehs-TRAHR-seh |
| Check out (from a hotel) | *Dejar el hotel* | deh-HAR el oh-TELL |
| Cheeks | *Cachetes* | cah-CHEH-tehs |
| Cheese | *Queso* | KAY-soh |
| Cherry | *Cereza* | sair-REH-szah |
| Chicken | *Pollo* | POH-zhoh |
| Chin | *Barbilla* | bahr-BEE-zhah |
| Chocolate | *Chocolate* | choh-coh-LAH-teh |
| Clerk | *Funcionario* | foon-see-oh-NAIR-ee-oh |
| Climate | *Clima* | CLEE-mah |
| Coat | *Chaqueta* | chah-KAY-tah |
| Coffee | *Café* | cah-FAY |
| Coffee shop | *Café* | cah-FAY |
| Cold (It's cold) | *Hace frío* | AH-say FREE-oh |
| Cougar | *Puma* | POO-mah |
| Cousin (male) | *Primo* | PREE-moh |
| Cousin (female) | *Prima* | PREE-mah |
| Cow | *Vaca* | VAH-cah |
| Cream | *Crema* | CRAY-mah |
| Cup | *Taza* | TAH-szah |
| Cycling | *Ciclismo* | see-CLEESZ-moh |

**D**

| | | |
|---|---|---|
| Daughter | *Hija* | EE-hah |
| Day | *Día* | DEE-ah |
| December | *Diciembre* | dee-see-IHM-breh |
| Dining room | *Comedor* | coh-meh-DOHR |
| Dinner | *Cena* | SAY-nah |
| Dog | *Perro* | PAIR-roh |
| Donkey | *Burro* | BOOR-roh |

**E**

| | | |
|---|---|---|
| Eagle | *Aguila* | ah-WEE-lah |
| Ears | *Oreja* | oh-REH-hah |
| Eggs | *Huevos* | HWAY-vohs |
| Eight | *Ocho* | OH-choh |
| Elevator | *Elevador, or ascensor* | ay-leh-vah-DOHR, ah-SEHN-soar |
| Eyes | *Ojos* | OH-hohsz |

**F**

| | | |
|---|---|---|
| Face | *Cara* | CAH-rah |
| Fall | *Otoño* | oh-TOH-nyoh |
| Father | *Padre, Papi* | PAH-dreh, PAH-pee |
| February | *Febrero* | feh-BRAIR-oh |
| Fingers | *Dedos* | DEH-dohsz |
| Fish (to eat) | *Pescado* | pehs-CAH-doh |
| Fish (in the water) | *Pez* | PEZZ |
| Five | *Cinco* | SEEN-coh |
| Football | *Fútbol americano* | FOOT-bohl ah-mehr–ee CAHN-oh |
| Fork | *Tenedor* | teh-neh-DOHR |
| Four | *Cuatro* | KWAH-troh |
| Fox | *Zorro* | ZOHR-roh |
| Friday | *Viernes* | vee-AIR-nehz |
| Friends | *Amigos* | ah-MEE-gohz |
| Fruit | *Fruta* | FROO-tah |

**G**

| | | |
|---|---|---|
| Gift shop | *Tienda de regalos* | tee-IHN-dah day reh-GAH-losz |
| Glass (drinking) | *Vaso* | VAH-szoh |
| Gloves | *Guantes* | HWAHN-tehs |
| Go (Let's go) | *Vámonos* | VAH-moh-nohsz |
| Goat | *Cabra* | CAH-brah |

| Gold | *Oro* | OH-roh |
| Golf | *Golf* | GOALF |
| Good | *Bueno* | BWAY-noh |
| Goodbye | *Adiós* | ah-dee-OHS |
| Good/well | *Bien* | bee-IHN |
| Grandfather | *Abuelo* | ah-BWAY-loh |
| Grandmother | *Abuela* | ah-BWAY-lah |
| Grandson | *Nieto* | nee-AY-toh |
| Granddaughter | *Nieta* | nee-AY-tah |
| Grapes | *Uvas* | OO-vahsz |
| Gray | *Gris* | GREESE |
| Green | *Verde* | VAIR-deh |
| Gymnastics | *Gimnasia* | heem-NAHSZ-ee-ah |

## H

| Hail | *Granizo* | grah-NEE-zoh |
| Hair | *Cabello* | cah-BEH-zhoh |
| Ham | *Jamón* | hah-MOHN |
| Hands | *Manos* | MAH-nohsz |
| Handkerchief | *Pañuelo* | pahn-WEH-loh |
| Hat | *Sombrero* | sohm-BRAIR-oh |
| Head | *Cabeza* | cah-BEH-szah |
| Helicopter | *Helicóptero* | ay-lee-COHP-tair-oh |
| Hello (greeting) | *Hola* | OH-lah |
| Hello (answering phone) | *¿Hola?, Alo* | OH-lah, AH-loh |
| Highway | *Camino* | cah-MEE-noh |
| Hips | *Caderas* | cah-DEH-rahsz |
| Hockey | *Hockey* | OH-kee |
| Horse | *Caballo* | cah-BAH-zhoh |
| Hot | *Caliente* | cah-lee-IHN-teh |
| Hot (It's hot— temperature) | *Hace calor* | AH-say cah-LOHR |
| Hotel | *Hotel* | OH-tehl |

| House | *Casa* | CAH-szah |
| Hundred | *Cien* | see-IHN |

## I–J

| I | *Yó* | YOH |
| Jacket | *Chaqueta* | chah-KAY-tah |
| January | *Enero* | ay-NAIR-oh |
| June | *Junio* | HOON-yoh |
| July | *Julio* | HOOL-yoh |

## K

| Kitchen | *Cocina* | coh-SEE-nah |
| Kitten | *Gatito* | gah-TEE-toh |
| Knife | *Cuchillo* | coo-CHEE-zhoh |

## L

| Lieutenant | *Teniente* | ten-ee-EHN-teh |
| Lips | *Labios* | LAH-byohsz |
| Lightning | *Relámpago* | ray-LAHM-pah-goh |
| Lobby (in a building) | *Vestíbulo* | vehs-TEE-boo-loh |
| Lunch | *Almuerzo* | ahl-MWAIR-szoh |

## M

| Ma'am | *Señora* | seen-YOHR-ah |
| March (month) | *Marzo* | MAHR-zoh |
| Maroon | *Granate* | grah-NAH-teh |
| May | *Mayo* | MY-oh |
| Midnight | *Medianoche* | may-dee-ah-NOH-cheh |
| Milk | *Leche* | LAY-chee |
| Million | *Millión* | mee-ZHON |
| Miss | *Señorita* | Seen-yohr-EE-tah |
| Monday | *Lunes* | LOON-ehz |
| Month | *Mes* | MACE |

| Last month | Mes pasado | MACE pah-SAH-doh |
| Nest month | Próximo mes | PROAK-see-moh MACE |
| Moon | Luna | LOO-nah |
| Moonlight | Luz de luna | LOOZ deh LOO-nah |
| More | Más | MAHSZ |
| Mother | Madre, Mami | MAH-dreh, MAH-mee |
| Mouth | Boca | BOH-cah |

**N**

| Napkin | Servilleta | sair-vee-ZHAY-tah |
| Neck | Cuello | KWEH-zhoh |
| Necktie | Corbata | cohr-BAH-tah |
| Nephew | Sobrino | soh-BREE-noh |
| Niece | Sobrina | soh-BREE-nah |
| Nine | Nueve | noo-AY-veh |
| Noon | Mediodía | may-dee-oh-DEE-ah |
| November | Noviembre | noh-vee-IHM-breh |
| Number | Número | NEW-mair-oh |

**O**

| October | Octubre | oak-TOO-breh |
| Okay | Bueno | BWAY-noh |
| One | Uno | OO-noh |
| Orange (color) | Anaranjado | ah-nah-rahn-HAH-doh |

**P**

| Pants | Pantalones | pahn-tah-LOH-nesz |
| Parents | Los padres | lohs PAH-drehs |
| Parrot | Loro | LOH-roh |
| Path | Senda | SEHN-dah |
| Peach | Durazno | doo-RAHZ-noh |
| Peanut butter | Mantequilla de cacahuate | mahn-teh-KEE-zhzh day cah-cah-HWAH-teh |
| Pepper | Pimiento | pee-mee-IHN-toh |

| | | |
|---|---|---|
| Pickup | *Camioneta* | cah-mee-oh-NEH-tah |
| Pig | *Cerdo* | SAIR-doh |
| Pillow | *Almohada* | ahl-moh-HAH-dah |
| Pink | *Rosado* | roh-SZAH-doh |
| Pistachio | *Pistacho* | pees-TAH-choh |
| Plate | *Plato* | PLAH-toh |
| Please | *Por favor* | POHR fah-VOHR |
| Potato | *Patata* | pah-TAH-tah |
| Purple | *Púrpura* | POOR- poor-ah |
| Purse | *Bolsa* | BOHL-sah |

## Q–R

| | | |
|---|---|---|
| Question | *Pregunta* | pray-GOON-tah |
| Rain (it's raining) | *Está lloviendo* | ess-TAH zhoh-vee-IHN-doh |
| Rain | *Lluvia* | ZHUH-vee-ah |
| Raincoat | *Impermeable* | eem-pehr-may-AH-bleh |
| Rainy | *Lluvioso* | zhuh-vee-OH-soh |
| Raspberry | *Frambuesa* | frahm-BWEH-sah |
| Ready | *¿Listo?* | LEES-toh |
| Red | *Rojo* | ROH-hoh |
| Restaurant | *Restaurante* | rehs-tah-RAHN-teh |
| Rice | *Arroz* | ah-ROSZ |
| River | *Río* | REE-oh |
| Road | *Camino* | cah-MEE-noh |
| Room | *Cuarto* | KWAHR-toh |
| Single room (in a hotel) | *Habitación* | ah-bee-tah-see-OHN |
| Double room (in a hotel) | *Habitación doble* | ah-bee-tah-see-OHN DOH-bleh |
| Room service | *Room service* | ROOM SAIR-veesz |
| Rose | *Rosa* | ROH-sah |
| Running | *Carrera* | cah-RAIR-ah |

# S

| | | |
|---|---|---|
| Sailing | *Vela* | VAY-lah |
| Salad | *Ensalada* | een-sah-LAH-dah |
| Salt | *Sal* | SAHL |
| Sardine | *Sardina* | sahr-DEE-nah |
| Saturday | *Sábado* | SAH-bah-doh |
| Scarf | *Bufanda* | boo-FAHN-dah |
| Sea | *Mar* | MAHR |
| September | *Septiembre* | sep-tee-IHM-breh |
| Seven | *Siete* | see-EH-teh |
| Sheep | *Oveja* | oh-VEH-hah |
| Ship | *Barco* | BAHR-coh |
| Shirt | *Camisa* | cah-MEE-sah |
| Shoes | *Zapatos* | szah-PAH-tohs |
| Shoulders | *Hombros* | OHM-brohsz |
| Sidewalk | *Acera* | ah-SEHR-ah |
| Silver | *Plata* | PLAH-tah |
| Sir | *Señor* | seen-YOHR |
| Sister | *Hermana* | air-MAH-nah |
| Six | *Seis* | SAYSZ |
| Skiing | *Esquí* | ess-KEE |
| Skirt | *Falda* | FAHL-dah |
| Skunk | *Zorrillo* | szohrREE-szhoh |
| Slow | *Despacio* | dehs-PAH-see-oh |
| Socks | *Calcetines* | cahl-seh-TEE-nehs |
| Son | *Hijo* | EE-hoh |
| Sorry, I'm sorry | *Lo siento* | LOH see-IHN-toh |
| Snack | *Refrigerio* | ray-free-HAIR-ee-oh |
| Snake | *Culebra* | coo-LEH-breh |
| Snow | *Nieve* | nee-EV-eh |
| Soup | *Sopa* | SOH-pah |
| Spoon | *Cuchara* | coo-CHAH-rah |
| Spring | *Primavera* | pree-mah-VAIR-ah |

| | | |
|---|---|---|
| Stomach | *Estómago* | ess-TOH-mah-goh |
| Storm | *Tormenta* | tohr-MEHN-tah |
| Strawberry | *Fresa* | FREH-sah |
| Stream | *Arroyo* | ah-ROY-yoh |
| Street | *Calle* | CAH-zheh |
| Sugar | *Azúcar* | ah-ZOO-cahr |
| Suit | *Traje* | TRAH-heh |
| Suite | *Suite* | SWEE-teh |
| Summer | *Verano* | vair-AH-noh |
| Sun | *Sol* | SOHL |
| Sunlight | *Luz del sol* | LOOZ dehl SOHL |
| Sunday | *Domingo* | doh-MEEN-goh |
| Sweater | *Suéter* | SWEH-tair |
| Swimming | *Natación* | nah-tah-see-OHN |

**T**

| | | |
|---|---|---|
| Table | *Mesa* | MEH-sah |
| Tablecloth | *Mantel* | mahn-TEHL |
| Tango | *Tango* | TAHN-goh |
| Ten | *Diez* | dee-AYSZ |
| Telephone | *Teléfono* | teh-LAY-foh-noh |
| Temperature | *Temperatura* | tehm-pair-ah-TOO-rah |
| Tennis | *Tenis* | TEH-neesz |
| Terrorist | *Terrorista* | tehr-roh-REE-stah |
| Thank you | *Gracias* | GRAH-see-ahs |
| Thousand | *Mil* | MEEL |
| Three | *Tres* | TRACE |
| Thursday | *Jueves* | HWAY-vehz |
| Tiger | *Tigre* | TEE-greh |
| Time | *Tiempo* | tee-IHM-poh |
| Time (What time is it?) | *¿Qué hora es?* | kay ORAH ess |
| Tired | *Cansado* | cahn-SAH-doh |
| Toast | *Tostada* | tohs-TAH-dah |

| | | |
|---|---|---|
| Today | *Hoy* | OY |
| Toes | *Dedos de pies* | DEH-dohsz day pee-AYSZ |
| Toffee | *Caramelo* | cah-rah-MEH-loh |
| Tomato | *Tomate* | toh-MAH-teh |
| Tomorrow | *Mañana* | mahn-YAH-nah |
| Day after tomorrow | *Pasado mañana* | pah-SAH-doh mahn-YAH-nah |
| Tongue | *Lengua* | LEN-gwah |
| Towel | *Toalla* | toh-AHL-lah |
| Truck | *Camión* | cah-mee-OHN |
| Tuesday | *Martes* | MAHR-tehz |
| Turquoise | *Turquesa* | toor-KAY-szah |
| Turtle | *Tortuga* | tohr-TOO-gah |
| Twelve | *Doce* | DOH-seh |
| Two | *Dos* | DOSE |

## U

| | | |
|---|---|---|
| Umbrella | *Paraguas* | pahr-AH-wahs |
| Uncle | *Tío* | TEE-oh |
| Undershirt | *Camiseta* | cah-mee-SEH-tah |
| Underwear | *Ropa interior* | ROH-pah een-tehr-ee-OHR |

## V

| | | |
|---|---|---|
| Vanilla | *Vainilla* | vy-ah-NEE-zhah |
| Vegetables | *Verduras* | vair-DOO-rahs |
| Violet (color) | *Violeta* | vee-oh-LEHT-ah |
| Volleyball | *Voleibol* | VOH-leh-ee-bohl |

## W

| | | |
|---|---|---|
| Waffle | *Wafle* | WAH-fleh |
| Wakeup call | *Servicio de despertador* | sair-VEE-see-oh day dehs-pair-tah-DOHR |

| | | |
|---|---|---|
| Wallet | *Billetera* | bee-zheh-TAIR-ah |
| Water | *Agua* | AH-wah |
| Weather | *Tiempo* | tee-IHM-poh |
| Wednesday | *Miércoles* | mee-AIR-coh-lehz |
| Week | *Semana* | seh-MAH-nah |
| Last week | *Semana pasada* | seh-MAH-nah pah-SAH-dah |
| Week before last | *Antesemana* | ahn-teh-seh-MAH-nah |
| Next week | *La próxima semana* | lah PROAK-see-mah seh-MAH-nah |
| Where are we going? | *¿A dónde vamos?* | ah DOHN-deh VAH-mohs |
| White | *Blanco* | BLAHN-coh |
| Windy (It's windy) | *Hay viento* | EYE vee-IHN-toh |
| Winter | *Invierno* | een-vee-AIR-noh |
| Wolf | *Lobo* | LOH-boh |
| Work | *Trabajo* | trah-BAH-hoh |
| Wrists | *Muñecas* | moon-YAY-cahsz |

## Y

| | | |
|---|---|---|
| Year | *Año* | AHN-yoh |
| Yellow | *Amarillo* | ah-mah-REE-zhoh |
| Yesterday | *Ayer* | ah-YARE |
| Day before yesterday | *Anteayer* | ahn-tay-ah-YARE |
| You're welcome | *De nada* | day-NAH-dah |

# COMING SOON

## *Eiffel's Trifles and Troubles:*
## *Les Chats of the C.I.A.*

Will *Capitán Ramos* succeed in his attempt to help *Carlos* the Puma escape from *PFA y Buenos Aires*? If they are successful, where will *Ramos* take *Carlos*? How much will *Carlos* pay the *capitán*? And where will *Carlos* go to resume his career as a terrorist?

Answers to these questions—and more—can be found in the sample from *Eiffel's Trifles and Troubles: Les Chats of the C.I.A.* on the pages that follow.

Available 2011 from Eakin Press

# Eiffel's Trifles and Troubles:
## Les Chats of the C.I.A.

# * Chapter 1 *
# The Great Escape

*En El Río de La Plata—Argentina*

*Capitán Ramos* ran his thirty-nine foot trawler *Meteoro* downstream toward the Atlantic Ocean from *Buenos Aires*— at night and without lights. He had been lucky so far. Taking the C-4 plastic explosives to *Carlos* the Puma at the headquarters of the *PFA—Policía Federal de Argentina*—in *Buenos Aires* had been the right thing to do. He was now sure of that. Helping the big puma escape from the authorities would pay off handsomely, he knew. *Carlos* is loaded, he told himself, and now he'll be grateful for my continued help, and he'll share a nice portion of that fortune with me. Soon I'll be rich.

*Ramos'* involvement with the international terrorist *Carlos* the Puma had begun only a week ago way up near the headwaters of the Amazon. *Carlos* had escaped from a dreadful prison near Brazil's borders with *Venezuela* and *Guyana*. The puma had paid *Ramos* a large sum of *pesos* to bring him to the mouth of the Amazon at the Atlantic.

Even though the puma had jumped ship before reaching the ocean, he'd still paid *Ramos* the full amount they had bargained for.

*Ramos*, in fact, had not known the name or identity of his passenger until hours before *Carlos* slipped over the side of the *Meteoro* and cat paddled to the south shore of the big river. There the puma had made his way to a secret landing strip in the middle of the rain forest and, from there, to *Buenos Aires* in his quest to get even with a black-and-white cat and the cat's friend, a dancing pig.

Before *Carlos* could confront his cat and pig adversaries, however, they had captured him as they worked with the *PFA* in a clever plot to put the puma back in prison.

*Carlos* slept below decks. *Ramos* would wait until he woke up to find out where the big cat wanted to go. After all, the major goal at the moment was just getting the trawler to the open waters of the Atlantic without being seen by the authorities.

*Ramos* knew he was into the thick of things up to his neck. Not even a clever story would save him if the police found *Carlos* on the *Meteoro*. Still, without allowing himself to lose concentration, *Ramos* began to think of how he could explain having an international terrorist on board if the authorities confronted him. An international terrorist who had just bombed a portion of the headquarters of the *PFA*. With plastic explosives that *Ramos*, posing as the puma's lawyer, had sneaked into the building in a small suitcase.

Almost silently, the *Meteoro* slid downriver with the current, in total darkness.

* * *

*Al Aeropuerto Internaciónal Ezeiza en Buenos Aires*

It was six in the morning on the tarmac outside Terminal C at *Buenos Aires'* big airport. Cincinnati the dancing pig had called ahead. His beautiful twin-fanjet Sabreliner was fueled and ready for the eight thousand kilometer trip back to the Texas Hill Country. Buzzer Louis, black-and-white tuxedo cat and Cincinnati's best friend, was talking softly at the cockpit door with his younger sister, Dusty Louise. Dusty, a pretty gray tabby, worked hard to overcome her natural tendency to be impatient. Part of her therapy involved learning to fly airplanes. She would help Cincinnati fly the Sabreliner, known as *The Flying Pig Machine*, back home to Texas . . . a long trip with a stop for fuel at *Guayaquil, Ecuador.*

Buzzer and Dusty's tiny orange tabby twin siblings, Luigi Panettone Giaccomazza and Luisa Manicotti Giaccomazza, pranksters of the first order who would normally be bundles of energy, slept huddled together under a buckled-up seat belt in the cabin. The capture of *Carlos* yesterday, followed by his unexpected escape, had made them tired.

Cincinnati, headphones in place, cued Dusty with a hoof pointed toward her as she sat in the right seat of the cockpit. She keyed the microphone clipped around her chin and spoke to the air traffic controller in the tower to her left.

"*Ezeiza* tower, this is Sabreliner seven zero niner niner alpha bound for Texas *en Los Estados Unidos,*[1] asking for taxi

---

1. Texas in the United States—in Spanish

instructions." Dusty knew all aircraft traffic control world-wide used English to communicate.

"Sabreliner niner niner alpha, proceed to runway eleven. Wind is from the northeast at six knots steady. Temperature is sixteen degrees Celsius. There is no traffic in the area, Sabreliner. You're cleared for takeoff. Safe trip," the controller responded.

Cincinnati looked at Dusty Louise. "You take it from here," he said much to Dusty's delight. There was almost no ground traffic so early in the morning and, although Cincinnati knew Dusty was still learning, little chance for danger in taxiing to the runway.

As the Sabreliner roared down the runway and into the sky on its way back to the Hill Country Intergalactic Airport and Buzzer's little ranch in the Texas Hills, Luigi Panettone Giaccomazza and his tiny twin sister, Luisa Manicotti Giaccomazza, woke from their nap and started begging their big brother Buzzer Louis for a story.

"Tell us a story, Buzzy, pleeeze," they asked. "Tell us about you and Cincinnati in Hong Kong when you captured that Chinese opium smuggler Ar-Chee the Panda."

* * *

*En el Bote Meteoro*

Before the sun came up, *Ramos* had the *Meteoro* out in the open waters of the Atlantic Ocean. He deliberately headed about eighty kilometers—fifty miles—off the Argentinean shore into open water. Just to avoid any *PFA* patrols. No use inviting a boarding. Besides, the sea was calm, and the trawler, with no freight, rode high in the water.

As the morning sun began to peep over the eastern horizon above the softly rolling, glassy surface of the Atlantic, *Carlos* the Puma, escaped international terrorist, woke from his sleep and wandered up from the below-decks cabin. He yawned and stretched casually, as if he didn't have a care in the world.

"Where are we, *Ramos*?" he asked the captain.

"We cleared the mouth of the *Río de La Plata* about four hours ago, *señor*, and we've turned northeast toward *Brasil*. I'm staying about eighty kilometers offshore in the open water to be sure we're not searched," *Ramos* answered.

"Where would you like me to take you?" *Capitán Ramos* asked the question that had been burning all night in the back of his mind.

*Carlos* thought for a minute as if doing some time and distance calculations in his head. Then he answered, "Remember the spot on the Amazon where I left your trawler last week?" he asked, recalling his escape as two *Brasileño policía* had boarded the *Meteoro* to look for a big puma who had just escaped from a terrible prison near the big river's headwaters.

*Ramos* nodded. "I know the spot, *señor*, the captain said with some certainty. "I don't think I'll ever forget that spot. I thought we both were goners when the *policía* came aboard."

"*Bueno*,"[2] *Carlos* said, adding, "Take me there, *Ramos*,

---

2. "Good" in Spanish

only this time closer to the shore. I have friends who'll pick me up there and take me on to my next job. The dratted *Norteaméricano*[3] cat and his pig friend will have to wait. But I'll get them. Count on it, *capitán*."

*Carlos* shaded his eyes with his right front paw and gazed out across the open water, adding almost to himself, "Yes, I will get them. Nobody crosses *Carlos* the Puma twice. Nobody!"

For *Ramos*, there was still unfinished business. Business that had brought him and the puma to where they were at the moment and where they would be going for the next several hours.

It was time to get down to that business.

"Our escape last night was close, *Carlos*," he said tentatively. "I risked much to come to your rescue, no? And now I risk even more smuggling you back to safety. Safety for you. Much danger for me."

*Carlos* looked at *Ramos* and smiled.

He said to the captain with almost a chuckle in his voice, "Why don't you just ask how much I'll pay you for your time and your risks, *Ramos*? Have I not been fair with you to this point? *Carlos* the Puma takes care of those who take care of him. So, *capitán*, you name your price, and I'll pay it. You know that *Carlos* has a lot of money, right? And that my next job will pay me even millions more *pesos*. Consider the risk to your boat and yourself and your future. And make the price worthy of that risk."

*Ramos* hadn't expected such a blank check. It confused

---
3. North American

him. Confused him so much he changed the subject to give himself time to think.

"Where will you go for your next job?" *Ramos* asked *Carlos*. "Is it somewhere where I can continue to be of service, *señor?*"

"Are you looking for a job, *capitán?*" *Carlos* asked. "You're a ship's captain. The captain of a fine trawler. A captain with a good business, *Ramos*. If I were you, after tomorrow I would forget I ever met *Carlos* the Puma. Take your new money—how much, again? And keep running up and down the big river."

*Carlos* thought for a minute, and then he added, "Your actions in freeing me from the *PFA* were frankly reckless. And foolish. I am grateful, of course. But *capitán*, you're not cut out to do the kind of work I do."

*Ramos* cringed.

And the price he'd quote the puma went up.

A lot.

\* \* \*

*In "The Flying Pig Machine" Over Bolivia*

"And so, Luigi and Luisa, that's how Cincinnati and I captured Ar-Chee the Panda in Hong Kong. And how I lost a claw from my front paw," Buzzer said, concluding a story that had taken almost two hours to tell as the little Sabreliner flew northwest toward its fuel stop at *Guyaquil* in *Ecuador*.

Luisa looked out the window at the tops of mountains peeping above puffy white clouds.

"Are we there yet?" she asked, causing Luigi to burst into laughter.

"Only kidding," Luisa added, smiling at Buzzer.

Just then Buzzer Louis' satellite phone rang.

"Buzzer Louis," he answered it. He listened for a minute, said "Yes" once and "No" twice and ended the conversation with "Sure, whatever."

"Who was that?" the ever-curious Luigi wanted to know.

"It was Socks in Washington, Luigi, the head of the C.I.A.—you know, Cats In Action. One of you run up to the cockpit and ask Cincinnati if he can come back here for a couple of minutes. We need to talk."

Luisa scampered forward, peeped into the flight deck and, quickly, Cincinnati followed her back into the cabin.

"What's up, Buzz?" the dancing pig asked.

Buzzer answered, "Socks just called. Seems her international monitoring satellite picked up a conversation between a ship somewhere in the South Atlantic and a cell phone in Argentina. Looks like our puma friend is likely headed to France.

"*Parlez vous Francais,*[4] Cincinnati?" Buzzer asked.

"*Oui, oui,*"[5] Cincinnati answered. "Let's gas up in *Ecuador* and plot a course to gay Paree."

---

4. "Do you speak French, Cincinnati?"
5. "Yes, yes."

## Other Books by George Arnold
## From Sunbelt Media

**The Cats of the C.I.A. Fiction Series**

*Get Fred-X: The Cats of the C.I.A.*
Recently retired as director of operations of the secret C.I.A. (Cats-In-Action), international crime fighting arm of the U.S. State Department run out of the White House basement by Socks, Buzzer Louis, world-renowned black-and-white tuxedo cat, has retired to the life of a gentleman farmer on a small ranch in the Texas Hill Country. One evening Fred-X, catnabbing owl and general all-around meanie, snatches Buzzer from his barn. Fred-X planned to fly him to Memphis. Along the way, Buzzer escapes and makes his way to Ohio to visit his old friend Cincinnati the dancing pig. But Fred-X won't give up. The owl follows Buzzer to Ohio and keeps trying to kidnap him. Buzzer and Cincinnati, with the help of a clever police sergeant and Cincinnati's very British butler, plot a diabolical plan not only to get Buzzer back home to Texas, but also to halt the catnabbing ways of Fred-X. Once and for all time.
They think.

*Hunt for Fred-X: Los Gatos of the C.I.A.*
Buzzer Louis, world-renowned retired director of operations of Cats-In-Action, climbs back into service at the request of former Mexican President Vicente Fox to help the Mexican national police (*Federales*) capture the infamous owl Fred-X, international villain and catnabbing meanie.

Fred-X is stealing cats in Mexico and flying them to the Yucatán to sell into slavery in Aruba. Buzzer takes along his old friend and C.I.A. contract operative Cincinnati the dancing pig, his pretty gray tabby sister Dusty Louise as interpreter, and his tiny orange tabby twin siblings—the very funny pranksters Luigi Panettone Giaccomazza and Luisa Manicotti Giaccomazza. On this international adventure that would make Tom Clancy envious, they all learn a little about Mexico, about Hispanic culture, and they learn to speak a little Spanish. You will, too. 750-word Spanish vocabulary incorporated into the text and in an extensive glossary/pronunciation guide.

### Fred-X Rising: I Gatti of the C.I.A.

Continuing the adventures of the clever and lovable cats from the Texas Hill Country, Buzzer Louis is summoned to Italy, this time by his first cousin, Césare Pepperoni Giaccomazza, who heads up the Rome bureau of Interpol. This time to track down once again that international catnabbing villain Fred-X. With the help of his German girlfriend Frieda-K and a greedy cardinal from the Vatican, Fred-X is grabbing Italian cats, taking them to Venice to a one-armed ship's captain who plans to sell them into the African slave trade. Buzzer heads for Italy, taking along his best friend Cincinnati the dancing pig, his pretty and impatient younger sister Dusty Louise, and—as interpreters—the hilariously funny tiny twin pranksters Luigi Panettone Giaccomazza and Luisa Manicotti Giaccomazza. Fighting the greedy forces of bad guys, they enlist the help of a band of Greek stunt cats on Italian motorcycles, a man with a wooden hand and *Il Papa*—the Pope, himself—in a clever plot to put an end to the owl's ugly ways. Once and for all time. As they track Fred-X across the Trentino they learn a little Italian history and culture and they learn to speak considerable Italian. You will, too. 750-word Italian vocabulary built into the text and an extensive glossary/pronunciation guide.

COMING SOON: *Eiffel's Trifles & Troubles: Les Chats of the C.I.A.*


**Nonfiction books for readers of all ages**

*Growing Up Simple: An Irreverent Look at Kids in the 1950s*
Foreword by Texas icon and humorist Liz Carpenter. This multi-award winning nonfiction novel is a fun and funny account of the incredible hijinks of a small band of merry pranksters, overachievers of the first order, who grew up in the placid, black-and-white world of the '50s, a time when life was simple. The only major fear most kids had to face was the ever-present threat of polio. Winner of the IPPY Humor Award from the Independent Publishers' Association as the funniest book published in North America in 2003; the Violet Crown Award from Barnes & Noble and the Writers' League of Texas as the best nonfiction book by a Texas author in 2003; and a coveted Silver Spur from Texas Public Relations Association. Critics call it a nonfiction Tom Sawyer made hilarious.

*Chick Magnates, Ayatollean Televangelist, &*
*A Pig Farmer's Beef: Inside the Sometimes Hilarious*
*World of Advertising*

A nonfiction novel, seriously funny and (almost) totally true, this book is the story of the amazingly off-the-wall and clever people of one of the Southwest's more creative advertising agencies between 1973 and 1998. It's living proof of how creativity, applied when least expected and always in unorthodox fashion, overcame almost any obstacle to the agency's and its clients' successes—clients like the chick magnates of Pilgrim's Pride Corporation, the surprisingly Muslim-like business practices of Reverend Pat Robertson's CBN, a larcenous Iowa pig farmer turned producer of some unbelievably nutritious beef, and many more. From otherworldly utility types at TXU to soft drink purveyor Pepsi Cola to both Dallas newspapers, Safeway's Tom Thumb supermarkets, super-Aggie Bum Bright, and a host of others. It's a business primer from the real world, where the rubber meets the road. Told in Arnold's confidential, talking-only-to-you storytelling style, a style reminiscent of Garrison Keillor, James Herriot and Mark Twain. Entertaining and informative even if you don't care a whit about advertising.

*BestSeller: Must-Read Author's Guide to Successfully Selling Your Book*

The truth, the whole truth and nothing but the truth about the author as marketer, presented with unprecedented humor and style. This book educates, inspires and occasionally frightens. Accompanied by 90-minute interactive workshop conducted by the author for writers' groups.

**For More Information Visit the Author's Website**
**www.CIAcats.com**

# About the Author

George Arnold began writing books following retirement from a thirty-two year career in the practice of marketing, advertising and public relations in Dallas. For the last twenty-five of those years, he was president and chief operating officer of one of the more creative agencies in the Southwest.

His two award-winning nonfiction novels—*Growing Up Simple* (2003) and *Chick Magnates, Ayatollean Televangelist, & A Pig Farmer's Beef* (2007)—have established a reputation for him as a storytelling humorist. He conducts workshops throughout the South for writers on book marketing, based on his popular how-to book, *BestSeller: Must-Read Author's Guide to Successfully Selling Your Book*.

*Tango with a Puma: Los Gatos of the C.I.A.* (2010—English/Advanced Spanish) is the fourth in his multi-lingual international adventure series. The first trilogy included *Get Fred-X: The Cats of the C.I.A.* (2009); *Hunt for Fred-X: Los Gatos of the C.I.A.* (2005—English/Spanish); and *Fred-X Rising: I Gatti of the C.I.A.* (2006—English/Italian). Plans for the second trilogy, in addition to *Tango with a Puma*, include introductions to both basic French and German.

George lives in Texas. He and his wife of more than forty-five years have four children and four grandchildren.

For more information, visit the author's website:

**www.CIAcats.com**

CPSIA information can be obtained at www.ICGtesting.com
Printed in the USA
BVOW08s2157220415

397381BV00007B/45/P